# TwentyFour7

## contemporary tales for people on the move

James Maher

*TwentyFour7*

ISBN 0-9554491-0-3
978-0-9554491-0-9

Published by
Showtime Publications
Easthampstead
Bracknell
Berkshire
England



A CIP catalogue record of this book can be obtained from the British Library.

Designed & produced by:
The Better Book Company Ltd
Forum House
Stirling Road
Chichester
West Sussex
PO19 7DN

Printed in England

## CONTENTS

*Page*

# ACKNOWLEDGEMENTS

I would like to thank the following people for their invaluable support and guidance in bringing TwentyFour7 to life:

Ruth for her endless patience, encouragement and support, and for never losing faith in me.

Mum for believing in me and pushing me to carry on regardless.

Nicola for the constructive feedback in the finest detail! I owe you for the cover!

My appreciation also goes to Sarah Feeley for putting my name (and work) into print, giving me an audience for the very first time.

Finally, thanks to you – if you have parted with some hard-earned cash to read this book, I am truly privileged and honoured – I hope you don't feel let down. Thank you.

*For Dad*

# *Maiden Victory*

She had waited her whole life for this moment – nothing would stand in her way. Even now, wracked with paralysing stage fright for the first time ever, nothing was going to deny her this moment, her place in history.

For such a grand occasion, the holding room was incredibly small. Cramped into its bland white walled confines were the four people that mattered most of all to her: Thomas, her husband of twenty-five years, Hannah, her twenty-one year old daughter, who, even now, was able to bicker with her younger brother by two years, Stephen. Finalising the quartet was her closest lifelong friend, confidante, personal secretary and style guru, Geraldine.

Analysing every detail of her appearance in the full-height mirror, it was easy to criticise every nuance of what her reflection directed back to her. Was the blue two-piece suit too dark, or too light? Had the white blouse been pressed correctly? Was her youthful blonde hair inch perfect? Was her lipstick applied evenly? In her own mind, the answer was always no.

'For goodness sake! You look awesome!' Geraldine reassured.

'Indescribably brilliant!' Thomas enthused.

'Well, what about you two? Does your Mum look the part or not?' She addressed the reflections of her two children, giving in to the illusion that she possessed "eyes in the back of her head" – something that one of her rivals had jokingly referred to on the trail – yet the description had stuck with her from that moment on.

'Honestly, Mum – you really do look fantastic!' Stephen sincerely gushed. Hannah even went so far as to say that she was actually proud of her mother.

Suitably calmed, she walked away from the clear glass, staying on her feet. Sitting down on the beige sofa in the corner with the others would surely crease her suit, a suit that would assume an iconic identity after today.

There was barely a minute now, until she would be called, her vocation about to be realised. Looking at her family before her now, it had all been worth it. Everything had been decided for her that awful day fifty-one years before. Fate had played a cruel hand in deciding her destiny. Being robbed of her father's life by an assassin's bullet had devastated the family, and yet, at the age of six, whilst waving a final goodbye to her daddy's casket, she decided that she would continue the work where he left off.

‘You OK Mum?’ Hannah brought her out of a time always remembered despite being best forgotten.

‘I’m fine. Never better. I was just thinking about your grandfather.’

Thomas approached her, gently placing his hand on her shoulder, validating everything with the words she had been desperate to hear. ‘He would have been so proud of you too, as we all are.’

In that moment, she absolutely knew it had all been worth it. All the thousands and thousands of miles, the endless, tireless campaigning for the cause, the litigation, the sleepless nights and most of all, the time lost being spent apart from the very people in this room now. As they all stood and embraced, a solitary tear of joy rolled defiantly down her cheek. ‘Thank you. Thank you so much,’ she whispered to them all.

Geraldine broke the moment, bringing them all back to reality again.

‘Once you hear that knock on the door, you become the property of the world at large. Today is your day. Enjoy it, savour it, then, get on with the business of picking up where your dad left off. Show the world there is no such thing as being too late. Do you understand?’

'Most definitely!' She grinned back, energised and ready for the challenges that lay ahead. Whilst it was never going to be easy being a woman working in a man's world, she had her own unique imprint to leave on it, starting today.

An abrupt, business-like, double knock at the door started the whole formal process. It was time.

'Come in.' She spoke softly, however, firmness in her voice clearly evident.

The two special services agents entered the room in one slick, fluid movement. Stepping forward one stride, the tallest addressed her directly.

'Mrs President? It's time ma'am.'

Turning to those she loved and trusted the most, one final hug and kiss for each of them, Karen O'Connell, thirty-second, and first ever elected female president of the country, left the room with her hand-picked bodyguards to make the short journey onto the rostrum to take the oath of allegiance. This very journey, at this very moment, her father had made fifty-four years earlier.

During the swearing-in ceremony, the eyes of four billion souls across the world, full of hope and optimism, shared her moment with her.

## *Revelations*

Lee's head was spinning with what had happened – the secret was out and things were getting totally out of control. He was slumped on the floor, sitting cross-legged, staring blankly at the palms of his hands.

'How can this be?' he whispered to himself, with equal measures of shock and horror dominating his voice. Considering events of the last seventy-two hours had placed the very foundations of his existence into question, his thought process still functioned, despite the confusion and pain.

Outside, beyond the strong, mahogany front door that he leant on to support him, the world was descending into anarchy and chaos. Fierce, dark storm clouds rumbled and clattered as lightning crackled and scorched its way to earth from the angry, unforgiving sky.

Rising above the racket of the thunderstorm was the constant banging on the door, punctuated with intrusive questions and demands from people who were complete strangers, yet knew *everything* about him.

'Mr Reynolds, will you give us a statement please?' was the most repeated request that penetrated the gloom.

'How do you feel about the confirmation? What do you wish to say on behalf of your family?' Many different voices, all of them jostling for position out there, yet none of them really *cared*.

'Leave me alone!' he bellowed back at them, fighting to control the tears that threatened to course down his face any second.

Inside, as another screaming flash of lightning ripped through the darkening evening sky, illuminating the interior of their home, Lee's parents sat together in the lounge, distressed beyond words, yet concerned beyond belief for their teenage son.

'Mr Reynolds, will you be offering yourself as a donor?' a female voice yelled through the letterbox.

Despite the heartbreaking distress caused by their current situation, the television was switched on to the national news, a strange yet tormenting form of additional company to guide them through this family crisis.

'Mum! Dad!' Lee yelled from his position in the front hallway. 'What shall I do? What do I tell them?' His only response was silence. His plea had fallen on deaf ears.

'MR REYNOLDS!' An anonymous mouth aggressively yelled through the door, 'Please! Just one quote and we will leave you alone! Please! Open the door and give us what we need!'

Somehow, he found enough energy to shut the voices out, pull himself upright, and, ever so slowly, made his way across the entrance hall, to join his parents. He was met by the sight of his mother sitting at one end of the battered old sofa, curled in the foetal position, crying uncontrollably, her breath catching with every sob. At the other end sat his father, face full of fury and hurt, staring intently at the news broadcast beaming into their home.

'Mum? Dad? Please, what should I do?' he pleaded, needing guidance.

'It's my entire fault! I should have told you both!' wailed his mother, devastated by guilt and shock.

'Dad? What do you think? How do I deal with them?'

Unable to look his son in the eye, let alone speak to him, Lee's father simply shrugged his shoulders, continuing to watch the unfolding drama of the news broadcast. It was as if he were defeated already, his eyes betraying the hurt he clearly felt inside.

Casting his own attention to the TV, there was no getting away from the nightmare Lee and his parents were living through right now. On the screen, broadcasting live, from outside the front of this very house, an energetic, high profile news reporter was updating the nation on the recent startling developments in the biggest news story of the year, possibly the decade.

Closing his eyes, in the hope it would at least slow down the turmoil in his mind, Lee decided there was no option. He would face the world, and inform everyone of his decision. There would be time later to clear up the mess. Time to evaluate his life, decide which path to take, with the help of his parents.

Keeping his eyes closed, taking a deep breath, he listened intently to the news bulletin:

'... As the King lies in an induced coma for a fourth day, a donor of the exact blood match has been found, albeit in the most shocking of circumstances. Mr Lee Reynolds, of the address behind me, has positively tested an exact DNA match to His Majesty, and been identified as a suitable donor. It is believed that Mr Reynolds is the product of a relationship between His Majesty and Mr Reynolds's mother some seventeen years ago ...'

Walking purposefully towards the front door, ready to tell the assembled media of his decision, Lee made a mental note to himself. When this was all over, he would need a long talk with his mother about keeping secrets ...

## *Conditions of Contact*

She shut her eyes. It was now or never. A brief moment of hesitation, then Gemma locked her car, wearily making her way through the dark, freezing concrete corridors of the car park exit. It was 4.30 am on a late November morning, and the lack of people at this hour, in this normally busy place, made her surroundings even more sinister and foreboding. Despite this, her sense of suspicion had been dimmed by the two hour drive that preceded arriving here.

As her footsteps echoed off the surrounding bare walls, Gemma again pieced together the fragments in her mind of the meeting about to happen within the next hour.

Ahead, the bright lights of the main building beckoned reassuringly, splintering the gloom, offering a hint of safety and wellbeing.

Slipping back into her mental well-formed outcome, she smiled to herself, visualising the point of contact, just as she had done so a million times over the past year. Hoping against hope this final meeting place would indeed provide her longed-for sense of self-purpose, Gemma made her way into the terminal building.

Ascending the main stairwell, obediently following bright yellow direction signs for the international arrivals lounge, the memories of the last twelve months occupied her mind.

It started with the sudden arrival of the letter, out of the blue, without warning. A distressed, emotionally shattering conversation with her mother revealed the truth behind its contents – all of which started her quest – leading to this unplanned destiny point.

Entering the arrivals lounge mimicked entering a whole new world within a world. The eerie, quiet isolation of the car park walkway, the shattering silence of the main concourse – aided by row upon row of closed shops, sparsely broken by the odd appearance of a determined cleaner – were erased as soon as she crossed its threshold.

Her first point of contact was the huge wall-mounted information board, telling her that the flight was on time, and that she was to proceed to waiting area C. Around her, a maelstrom of people bustled and jostled at the greeting ramps, eager to be in situ at the right time, to meet their loved ones as they arrived from their far remote destinations. The long hauls from

Sydney and Hong Kong had already landed, their beaming, smiling suntanned occupants spewing forth through the large white double doors, into the welcoming arms of those they had once left behind.

Queues formed within the demise of every shop occupying the vast lounge, the longest being reserved for those in the beaureaux de change, hire car booths and international newspaper kiosks.

As she had a little time to wait before the arrival of her inbound flight, Gemma joined a small queue of four people in one of the seemingly never-ending coffee shops dotted here, there and everywhere.

Preparing the correct money in her hand, the first pangs of nervousness prodded her heart, prompting it to speed up, her breath quickening slightly. Two men in front of her were chatting animatedly, complaining about the 'obscene time of the day' but that the 'going rate for the job was the best they were likely to get.' Listening intently, controlling her breathing, their conversation provided an ideal diversion to her own sense of agitation. However, when, through their ongoing complaining they identified themselves as chauffeurs, waiting for several occupants from the flight that she too had driven halfway across the country to meet, her heartbeat quickened once again.

Coffee could wait. Gemma fled from the queue, head down, needing her own piece of space to regroup as quickly as possible. Finding a nearby metal rail to cling onto with both hands, she again scanned the arrivals board. Its message was immortal, possibly life-changing. Her inbound flight from Auckland had landed.

Hurriedly making her way to section C, she had no further time to think, other than gaining a good vantage point.

Tentative telephone conversations followed, acknowledging the letter. Relationships were formed – albeit at a great distance – and confidences gained. Then, three months ago, the photograph provided the catalyst to arranging this momentous meeting. Gemma's only act of defiance had been refusing to reciprocate her father's gesture. After all, he had had thirty-six years since leaving her and mum to fend for themselves, sacrificing their wellbeing for a new life alone on the other side of the world.

He entered the packed meeting area, aged, weary and uncertain, looking for a lost daughter he had instigated contact with, yet, even now, with no photograph to validate, having no idea where Gemma was, or even if she was here.

Gemma, however, had decided.

'Dad! Dad!' Arms waving furiously, tears of joy trickling down her cheeks, she raised his photo for him to see.

## *Hubris*

The text message proved everything. It was a smoking gun in her eyes. How could she have been so foolish?

There was no mistaking the words contained in the message. Its content, nothing short of explosive – the manner in which it had fallen into her hands, sinister and dishonest – somehow a little too easily. Hindsight was a wonderful thing.

Caroline Craven was everything you would expect of a young family solicitor. Driven and ambitious with rapier intelligence and a huge point to prove in a male dominated environment. She had represented the best interests of her clients, usually messy divorce cases, for nearly five years.

Still only twenty-eight, she was well on course to achieve her goal of becoming a partner at Brampton Pickwell Associates by the time she was thirty.

Everything changed forever the day Rosemary Sanderson arrived at the office, having booked a free thirty minute consultation. During that initial conversation, Rosemary made it clear she was seeing Caroline on the recommendation of a friend, a former client.

Nothing strange there, this was normal practice within the business. Rosemary's case was big – the kind of case that would attract major local media attention, including high profile colleagues who would be representing the estranged husband, Jonathan Sanderson MP, Chief Secretary to the Treasury.

In the heated anticipation of the moment, Caroline accepted the case instantly, unusual for such a guarded young woman in a cut-throat profession. If she had been a little less eager to accept, she may have explored further as to why Rosemary was reluctant to share who the friend was making the recommendation that Caroline was indeed "the one".

Contracts were drawn, fees agreed, retainers paid.

Derrick Brampton, founder and senior partner of the firm, whilst delighted at such a strong high profile case, tempered Caroline with a word of warning when granting her wish of "first representation".

'This one will consume you. It will take over your mind, heart, body and soul. Be ready for that, but don't sell your soul to get the result you want. Do you understand?'

At the time, Caroline had been outraged at the suggestion.

From the outset, she immersed herself in the case. Representing the wife of such a prominent local figure – even if it was yet another sleazy, dishonest politician who came two a penny these days – was going to be a major credit on her CV. If a partnership wasn't forthcoming following this major victory, other firms – far and wide – would soon know her name. She was going to maximise this one for all it was worth.

Deep into the fifth week of proceedings, the heavy guns of Jonathan Sanderson's representation started firing back. They obviously did not approve of a fly in their expensive ointment, a female fly at that! Caroline was in her element. She had her target in her sights, and was not going to stay quiet for anyone. When the city found out their honourably elected member of the House was *not* the unassuming family man the media portrayed him as, but a deeply dishonest, immoral individual who had a penchant for dalliances with other like-minded men, the outrage and disbelief would be quite something else.

Into the seventh week, and the first prelim hearing loomed ever closer. The local press were apparently becoming "warm" to a rumour of marriage problems between Jonathan and Rosemary Sanderson.

On the morning of the prelim hearing, arriving slightly late due to an accident on the inner distribution road, a small white envelope sat atop Caroline's cluttered desk. Her name was written in childlike block print, as if scrawled in a rush, or, by someone with a limited grasp of literacy, marked "for your eyes only". Her suspicion was immediate, yet she rushed with impatient fingers that trembled slightly as she opened it.

'This had better be good ...' she muttered under her breath, not in the mood for pranksters, yet sensing a significant *something* about this particular letter – or whatever it was.

All that was contained within slipped out and gracefully floated to the floor. Picking up the tiny unsigned note, written in the same handwriting, she read its contents, and, in a state of elation, decided to comply with its written request.

Unbelievably, an as yet unknown source was requesting a meeting at 9.30 am in the green across the main plaza, promising absolute evidence of proof in the Sanderson case.

It was too good to be true.

Glancing over her shoulder to the digital wall-mounted clock, she knew that she had no time to waste. It was 9.24 and it would take at least three minutes to arrive at the rendezvous point. Ignoring the unreliable lifts to take her to ground level, she began the frenzied descent of the stairs from the eighth floor.

Rushing to the green with seconds to spare, her breath came in short painful gasps, yet she was determined to project an image of calm and professionalism, no matter who she was about to meet. Composing herself by sitting on the graffiti strewn bench, she did not have long to wait.

At the main entrance to the green, a tall young man shuffled through the creaking gate. Realising that she was alone, her heart skipped a beat as the first pangs of apprehension and uncertainty gripped her sense of reality.

The stranger was dressed in tatty, unclean casual clothes, face obscured by a hoodie. From this distance, Caroline was not sure if the ever-closer approaching stranger was male or female. Shuffling up to her, a gruff, inarticulate male voice abrasively made a form of introduction.

'You Caroline the solicitor bird?' he asked.

She was petrified now, yet determined not to show her uncertainty to this urchin, whatever hole he had crawled out from under.

'Yes.' She spoke firmly, defiantly. 'Who would like to know?'

'Don't matter love. But you may be interested in this.'

He thrust a mobile phone at her face. She nearly gagged at the blackened, grimy state of his fingernails. For a split second, this was the only thing her repulsed mind could concentrate on.

He placed the phone in her reluctant, mildly shaking hand. Fighting the urge to gag, Caroline concentrated on simply *not* touching the hand that presented her with the evidence. Evidence she was fully aware would guarantee her future in the legal business.

'Proof. Just read the latest text. No password needed. It belongs to an ex-boyfriend of Sanderson.' His gruff guttural voice had diluted in her senses – it was the content that was igniting the fireworks in her mind. Proof! In her hand, right here and now!

'£200 please.'

Her ecstasy was temporarily halted by the revolting demand of this animal before her. No matter what, he was of no use to anyone now, so why pay him? However, she was alone, and he seemed the type who would have no remorse at slitting someone's throat for the price of a cup of tea or a cigarette.

'Will a signed IOU do?' she heard herself say.

'Fine. As long as I get the money today. Just hurry up, I 'aven't got all day,' he barked impatiently, forcing her to judder slightly. He was probably in a rush to get his next fix she thought to herself, as she kept a tight hold of her newly acquired purchase.

Carefully placing the phone in her handbag, she removed a loose yellow post-it and a biro from the depths of the assorted mess and nonsense she kept in it. Quickly, she scribbled an IOU, writing a second – more densely populated – meeting place for later in the day, before authorising it with her signature.

'Ta.' The unseen informant shuffled off, out of the green, far quicker than when he entered.

Her heart raced as she switched the phone on. The intrusive electronic "ping" immediately informed her that a new text message had arrived. Moving the menu cursor to "open", she clicked to read the message. Her blood froze, as she took in the words before her.

'Caroline. I warned you about not selling your soul. J Sanderson is married. To Nicola. There is no affair. You have failed the partnership test. Come back to the office and collect your belongings. You are fired. Derrick.'

## *Sibling Rivalry*

He saw the car coming straight for him and yanked his steering wheel to the right.

Heart rapidly pumping ice through his veins, Robin braced for impact as the silver saloon scorched past, missing by a hair's width. He had avoided catastrophe in the nick of time. Forcing his own car into an opposite lock skid, relying on wits, willpower and sheer luck, he managed to avoid a monumental collision with any sort of immovable force, yet the screeching and scratching of metal tearing, tangling and twisting against the dense hedgerows of the narrow country lane brought strong nausea to the back of his throat.

Bringing his damaged estate to a standstill, he had no time to think about his near miss – or was that near hit? Looking into the rear view mirror, the driver of the silver car had braked hard, slamming it into reverse, tyres burning, screaming its way backwards up the lane towards Robin.

Inside, the deliberate actions of its driver were fuelled with fury and hatred.

Engaging first gear, Robin pressed the throttle with a sudden forceful movement, causing the tyres to scream their anger as, violently, the car jolted forwards. Everything in his capability to avoid collision with this kamikaze attacker was needed. He could not afford to be overtaken again, allowing this lunatic the chance to move further down the lane, turn around, and suicidally drive straight at him once more.

Moving rapidly through the gears, reaching dangerous speeds, Robin managed to distance himself temporarily from his attacker. Staying calm, he knew it wouldn't be long before his brother, Kevin, the silver car's driver, would reach the passing point in the lane, manoeuvre his car, face the right way again, and be back on Robin's rear bumper in no time.

Thinking quickly, Robin knew six miles of narrow, twisting lanes needed navigating before he emerged at the main road junction. For Kevin to reach him would be catastrophic. Innocent people would be hurt or killed. No, he would simply have to take control of the situation, without allowing his younger brother to take their lives in the process.

Killing the engine, he freewheeled the estate into the next available grass verge. Stepping out from the car, he caught sight of the extensive body damage to his vehicle. It was not pretty, but nowhere as horrendous as it would be if Kevin achieved what he set out to do twenty minutes ago.

In the near distance, only a mile and a half away, he heard the screeching of the sudden application of brakes, followed by frenzied wheel spinning as Kevin manoeuvred his much more powerful vehicle to face the right direction to carry out his mission.

Robin calmly walked into the centre of the lane, stopping just short of the blind corner his brother would encounter in the next two minutes. It was a scorching late July day, sun blazing in an azure blue sky. Not even the faintest of breezes existed to help with the stifling heat. The only accompanying sounds were the choir of sparrows in a nearby oak tree, and the ever-louder rage of an overheating engine, being driven to its absolute limits by a man blinded by anger and hurt.

This course of action was extreme Robin thought as he stood there, beads of sweat forming on his upper lip, sweat trickling down his bare back. It was also potentially suicidal.

However, the situation was so bad, this was the only way he would stop his younger brother killing himself or innocent others. After all, this was his entire fault anyway.

Pursuing his secret habit of the last eight months, Robin had finished his window cleaning round early, his last call of the day a discreet trip to Kevin's house on the other side of town.

These weekly visits, however, were not due to brotherly love. They were more of the sister-in-law love kind, as Robin had found himself caught up in a passionate, all consuming affair with his sister-in-law of eight years, Florence. How it had started was all a blur, and right now, it didn't matter; only that she had started it, and Robin had happily responded.

As with most deceptions, the deceiver and the deceived will at some point cross paths. Twenty minutes ago, theirs crossed in the most catastrophic way, when Kevin, having taken a half day from his successful banker's job in the city, made the life changing discovery of finding his wife and brother together in his own house.

Standing naked, eyes closed at the apex of the blind corner, seconds from the end of the chase, Robin was most ungrateful that the only item he picked up as he fled the crime scene was his car key.

# *Sins of the Father*

Oh, this is ridiculous, thought Jack. And he finally plucked up the courage to tap the figure on the shoulder.

Such an act of bravery in the crowded store, packed with eager shoppers, was a novelty for him. Usually he avoided engaging strangers at all costs. To him, they were simply a waste of time and energy.

The daunting figure ahead had been haunting him for several days. An uninvited guest, invading his mind, draping his waking hours with a dark cloak of uncertainty – the identity of this person *had* to be known.

Why right here and now, Jack was unsure. What he did know though, was that urgency was needed to dismiss this figure from his mind for once and for all.

Rubbing sore, tired eyes, having been deprived of sleep for five nights, he kept his mind clear, focusing on the job in hand.

Just what the trigger point had been was shrouded in uncertainty. His network of memories would forever hold back the secret that caused this "dark man" of Jack's dreams to manifest itself in such a brutal manner.

A young, successful manager for a blue chip insurance organization, he had always believed in the motto "work hard, play hard." For Jack, it was not just a catchphrase – it was a way of life.

No family burdened him at home. He lived in a small terrace within walking distance of the office. His determination limitless, a combination of sparkling intellect and ruthless ambition had catapulted him to a senior position in record time, making him the envy of many.

What he *did* remember was the drunken evening when the dark, menacing figure entered his life. It was two months ago; he had waited for Jack outside his home, shrouded underneath the nearby streetlight. He had the height and frame of a well-built man, yet stood perfectly still.

Senses dimmed by his inebriation, following a raucous evening to celebrate the signing of a new corporate client, Jack paid no attention to the looming figure opposite.

At the time, Jack was concentrating and fumbling to get his front door key to fit into the lock. He hardly noticed the stranger had moved to the end of his short garden path, let alone register that it spoke to him through the late night gloom.

'I'm ashamed of you.'

He remembered turning towards his visitor at the exact moment the key sank into the lock, and, as he lunged uncontrollably through the door, he had a vague memory of the figure sauntering into the shadows beyond.

Waking up stiff and sore on his lounge floor the next morning, Jack was far too concerned about his debilitating hangover to bother himself about his evening encounter.

As the day wore on, hangover cured, he went about his business as normal.

Only that night, his dreams changed.

Subtle and unassuming at first, the dark man gradually crept more and more into Jack's lucid visions of childhood memories. These dreams were commonplace for Jack, as his childhood had been extremely happy, excepting one notable relationship.

The dark man visited every night, taking a leading role in Jack's private theatre. Reaching out to him, never revealing his hidden face, yet beckoning Jack to change his ways. As the visions continued, the dark man gradually began taking the place of his father through his actions, words and deeds. Throughout the escalation of his appearances, the dark man never revealed his true self.

Being thick skinned, Jack always dismissed the dreams, basing himself solely in his ruthless, materialistic world of reality.

Until five days ago. Monday morning's routine was shattered by the figure of his dreams waiting for him at the entrance to his office block.

'You're no son of mine,' it whispered, face hidden by the scarf and hat it always wore.

Then it was gone.

Jack could not shake the image from his mind all day. For the first time in a very long time, doubt and uncertainty crept into his mind. That night, there were no dreams, sleep eluding him as he mentally replayed the words of the dark man.

For the next four mornings, the pattern was repeated. Despite desperate attempts to ignore his early morning greeter, yesterday, he had responded.

'You're not for real,' he whispered. 'Ghosts don't exist.' Then he ran home, back to another sleepless night.

Now was the time. He had noticed the figure straight away upon entering the store this morning. Bounding through the mass of shoppers, Jack now forcibly slapped his hand on the shoulder of his tormentor, spinning him round.

This time, there was no mistaking the identity. The face and voice were instantly recognisable.

'You're not for real, ghosts don't exist,' his father hissed.

As he passed out in shock, Jack remembered the final conversation he ever had with his father. It had been fifteen years earlier, on a dark and twisted night, where fate had collided with history in brutal fashion.

For that was the night he rejected Jack as a son, completely and finally. Within one hour of banishing him, Jack's father had died in his sleep, leaving the bonds of this earth with a shattering legacy for his son, forever beyond repair.

## *An Eye for an Eye*

Everywhere Marty turned seemed strange. Was he losing his mind or lost in some alternate universe.

Everything about the place he now stood in was familiar in every detail. 'The Blue Anchor' had been his local watering hole for the past decade, for all the right reasons too. He was amongst friends – convenient, safe and cosy.

Since frequenting the establishment, very little had changed. The clientele (many of whom Marty counted as close friends), were reassuringly, the same – night in, night out – and most importantly, the landlord and bar staff, amazingly, had remained unchanged throughout.

So, despite being surrounded by his good companions in a place he often referred to as his living room,  first waves of panic and apprehension began smothering his conscious thinking as the strangeness of the situation took a turn for the worst.

It was bad enough that no one had made any particular effort to speak to him tonight, leaving him alone in the corner with a broken fruit machine – still waiting for repair since the day he walked in. Conversations left hanging in the air last night remained unfinished. Bar staff he knew so well treated him with indifference.

Only now, as the burgundy and gold vertical striped walls began to imperceptibly wither and wave around him, did Marty question his mental wellbeing. After all, it was impossible for him to have been infiltrated here, this safest of places.

"Amongst friends" was an important turn of phrase in Marty's existence. For him, it meant being in the presence of like-minded souls, pursuing life fulfilment. For the regulars of 'The Blue Anchor', this meant crime – organized crime – of the most savage kind.

All of them, bar staff included, were interconnected in a complex web, hidden with many trails, virtually impenetrable, impossible to comprehend from the outside. United in cause, these professional colleagues, worked for the same dangerous figure, known to them as the mysterious, highly revered "Angel".

Just who "The Angel" was, no one knew, or cared to know. All they understood was that three trusted lieutenants knew the true identity, and rumour circulated they were prepared to die rather than hand that identity to the authorities.

Dazed and even more confused, Marty gripped the top lip of the gaming machine through sweaty palms to keep him upright. To his left, the pool table seemed to be stamping its legs to the muted, muffled music emanating from a jukebox that sounded as if under water.

What had happened? No one seemed to be aware of his *existence* right now; despite the obvious distress he must be seen to be in. Desperately reaching out for a shred of mental reality, Marty closed his eyes, aware of the weakness consuming his body, yet determined to recall if there was any way he had been compromised here, tonight.

Despite the security and seclusion of the circles they operated in, the previous twelve months had been difficult for the regulars of 'The Blue Anchor'. One by one, as if knowing in advance by local authorities, several of them had been apprehended in the process of their "day job", which amounted to anything from extortion to drug running.

Nervousness and agitation had become normal during the following months, and with it suspicion. Following one particular apprehension and conviction, the dictate from "The Angel" was clear.

Within their trusted ranks, an informer lurked. Silent and unseen, creating havoc, threatening to destroy the very fabric of their existence, he was amongst them, plotting treachery and betrayal.

On the ground, this declaration had been met with a strong sense of disbelief and incredulity. Many felt the leader was possibly too far distant and remote to understand the magnitude of such an allegation. Their brotherhood was far too tightly knit for such an allegation.

"The Angel" must be wrong.

Feeling his grip loosen, Marty could not prevent himself slowly sliding down the darkened side of the fruit machine. The floor beneath him had now taken on a life of itself, churning, twisting and thrashing, waiting to welcome him into a crescendo of perpetual movement.

His last conscious thoughts, as clear as a crystal sky, were processed as he sank to his knees, waiting for the end.

Marty was not going mad or suffering a breakdown, far from it. He had been infiltrated himself. Unbeknown to him, his *true* movements and motives had been identified. It all made sense now. It had all been a game after all. They *did* know he was the informer, every single one of them.

World rapidly fading, shrinking to the size of a white dot like a television shutting down, he was joined by Oona, the landlady.

Cradling his head, his last memory was the whispered words in his ear.

'Never trust the rage of an Angel Marty. I'll always win in the end.'

## *Hide and Seek*

There was no way back. Molly had been well and truly rumbled. She blinked into the spotlights, picked up the microphone and cleared her throat.

Around her, the thick acrid fog of exhaled cigarette smoke from the sold-out audience rasped her vocal chords and stung her eyes. In addition, the darkened gloom of the tiny working men's club was all too obvious, swallowing her whole.

Right now, Molly actually wished for that darkness to envelope her, taking her away from here, removing her from the consequences of actions carried out a lifetime ago, in another world.

Her introduction from the MC was met with the usual rapturous applause and cheering from the expectant sold-out audience. She was the reason so many travelled so far to pay so much money to see. Ever since her arrival, she had been a sensation, sparking excitement and a word of mouth "grapevine" unlike anything experienced before in these parts.

Molly stood, hunched and buckled, on the twelve foot square step that doubled up as the main stage every weekend night. For the last eleven months, she was the one the crowds had flocked to see. She was the main attraction, the star of the show, the girl whose name was on everyone's lips, the next "big thing." When she became a global superstar, Molly was going to put this place on the map.

Except tonight, their "Southern Sparrow" – as she had been affectionately christened by the appreciative local audience – had lost her singing voice. By the look of her, she had lost everything.

Awkward fidgeting preceded uncomfortable murmurings amongst the crowd. What was wrong with her? Why was she just stood there, trapped in the spotlights? Had she seen a ghost?

'Do you have stage fright love?' a burly steelworker in the third row from the front bellowed coarsely. His challenge met by nervous laughter from the gathered mass in the rows of occupied seats.

Molly didn't hear. Panic and uncertainty gripped her heart, freezing her blood as it ran through her veins. All she could focus on were the occupants of the three chairs immediately before her, the VIP row. Such was her paralysis; the slow handclapping and controlled jeering from beyond did not register.

How had they found her? Her escape had been so meticulously planned and executed. Months and months of scheming had gone into breaking away from them and starting again.

Aided by two of her closest confidants, Molly had successfully made her bid for freedom twelve months ago. Her course of action had been decided as a consequence of the failure of the system to deal with cases such as hers.

Within three hours, news of her escape leaked, making its way to the highest level in the chain of authority. The hunt began immediately – she was a high risk target, and, in the interests of safety and security – must be found at all costs.

Unaware of the frantic levels of energy and resource being invested in tracking her down, Molly had escaped to the North, ably assisted with false documentation coupled with determination to succeed.

Once tasting her freedom, Molly was determined to gain her life back as fully as possible, despite not officially existing.

This very determination had brought her here, to her sanctuary.

As the three dark faceless men rose from their chairs, Molly's last rational thought was of the day she arrived, banging forcefully on the tradesmen's entrance, hopefully clutching the small press advertisement to her chest.

The three men walked onto the stage. Booing and jeering reaching a crescendo as the audience saw the uniformed strangers reach out to their starlet in the making. From the furthest recess of the club, a small ashtray was hurled in the direction of the uninvited intruders.

Molly gave herself unto them without resistance, still visualising her first moments here, moments to treasure forever. She saw herself begrudgingly ushered in through the kitchens, onto the empty, soulless stage by the owner, Raymond. She remembered the thrill of singing for him unabated, as a free spirit. The never to be forgotten excitement as she signed a contract with him there and then, elevating her status to that of professional singer.

That was all gone now. They had found her, now consequences had to be paid. The price was worth it, for in the last year, she had fulfilled the ambition of a lifetime, and used her God-given talents to make a living.

As the three military policemen marched her from the building, pre-organized riot police moved in, controlling the anger and outrage.

Following being unceremoniously bundled into the army escort vehicle, Corporal Molly Savage, deserter, was read the list of charges against her. She stopped listening after the first charge of AWOL was read aloud, and looked to the future instead.

## *Sense of Reality*

The full moon lit the landscape, allowing the group to see as if it was day. The leader ushered the others towards the clearing in the woods. Finally they were able to rest ...

With their lungs burning from the excruciating effort made to get here, relieved sighs and groans filled the hitherto silent night sky as all six members of the patrol relieved themselves of their heavy kitbags that had burdened them for so long. Simultaneously, half a dozen forty-pound backpacks fell to the mossy ground with a whispered thud.

It had been a long time coming, reaching this particular point in the mission, probably too long. Leader one remained standing upright, senses alive, anticipating unseen danger in the wilderness around them.

As the single shaft of moonlight continued providing illumination for the group, he surveyed the landscape for the first time. For the last six hours, they'd manoeuvred through the dense growth under a sky as dark as a raven's wing. He was grateful and relieved in equal measures for the orientation point presented to them, allowing this chance of recuperation and reorganization.

All six of his command were sitting or lying down, massaging aching limbs and muscles. Despite intensive practice for such an event as this, the mission had been exhausting, the dense darkness adding to the debilitating effect on energy levels.

Fortunately, there had been no casualties thus far, something leader one was silently grateful for as he continued to scan their immediate surroundings.

They were gathered in a perfect spotlight of flattened scrub, 30–40 feet in diameter. Surrounding them, dark, thick bushes and trees, all intertwined with unforgiving thickly barbed thorn bushes, swallowed the world. In short, nothing more than a savage wilderness. Their perfect piece of light, their sanctuary, didn't illuminate the safest path out of here. That choice would have to be made by someone else.

Clearing his throat to address his men, the shaft of moonlight visibly shrunk, now offering a spotlight around them of half the size when they first arrived. Almost instantaneously, the dense bushes claustrophobically closed around them, as if choking the light from their world of darkness.

Despite this, leader one remained calm. As his men regrouped, standing to attention around him, without concern in their eyes, he relayed the current state of play to them in a cool, calm monotone, betraying no emotion. Weakness would only cause more problems.

'We have reached a point of no return. From here on in, we will have to face an enemy the likes of which we have never experienced *ever* before.'

As he spoke, the first rustlings from outside their circle of light interrupted him. Their quarry was already close, but, significantly, *they* were on *its* territory now. By reaching this patch of brightness in a dark and sinister place, everything had changed.

The advantage of familiar ground had been lost. The hunters had now become the hunted. Ignoring the distraction, leader one concluded his brief address.

'There is no wisdom or knowledge in my head that I can share with you to get us through this. Everything we have been trained for in the past has been achieved. Now, we face an unknown enemy with an uncertain character. We will move on from this place in the next few seconds, and it could all be over for us within a matter of seconds too ...'

Silence prevailed all around. There was no hint of emotion on any of their faces, despite the graveness of the situation.

'In all likeliness, the odds are against us. All we can do now is await our instruction for direction, and, when we get it, we do as we were trained – we follow it without question …'

Swallowing hard, leader one briefly deviated from his mental script.

'Finally, I just want you to know that I am proud to have worked with you, and proud to have served you as your leader.' There was a slight pause, followed by his formal finishing of the script.

'Does everyone understand?' he bellowed.

'Yes Sir!' they roared defiantly.

'Then we await our order of direction, and we deal with our fate like men …'

Before he finished the sentence, along came the final order for direction.

It came authoritatively, from far beyond the darkness and the gloom, millions of miles from the suffocating reality of the final journey for the group.

From the comfort of his bedroom, sat quietly at his desk, fourteen-year-old Nathan

Wilson took grip of his computer console joystick following a brief break to gather his wits.

In two years of trying, he had finally reached the final level of "Thrash", the most realistic computer combat simulation ever created. For the first time ever, he guided leader one plus team to new and unseen challenges within the confines of his monitor screen.

'OK. Let's go ... *this* way ...' he whispered excitedly to himself.

# *The Mirror Man*

As they set sail, the horizon beckoned them towards a new future. But Martin sensed he could never truly escape from the last few months.

When given the news of his appointment three months ago, his excitement had known no limits. For the first time in his career, he had the professional opportunity to show everyone what he could really do.

Now, gazing to nowhere, Martin remembered just how ecstatic he felt as Steven, his line manager, gave him the good news.

He also felt the unnerving wisdom of Steven's additional comments given to him on that fateful day as a sense of perspective. Grinning inwardly, he repeated out loud the sentence that was supposed to ground him in readiness for the job ahead:

'One day you will remember this moment, as if you were standing alone on a shore, with your head in the clouds and your pockets filled with dreams ...'

There was more, and, as his words bounced around the confines of the holding area, Martin supposed that Steven was a fortune teller, or, as he now realised, had been through all this before, probably with countless others.

Suddenly, cramp gripped his right calf, sending searing shards of pain through his leg, towards his chest. The pain was colossal, indiscriminate, and, like many other aspects of this assignment, to be expected.

Shifting uncomfortably in agony he tried unsuccessfully to massage the offending leg back into a contented state, but it was no good. Gasping in frustration, he laid back on the floor of the holding container, being careful not to wake the passengers crammed in either side of him. For that matter, so densely packed in were they, he did not wish to further disturb any of his five hundred travelling companions.

Closing his eyes tightly to shut out the pain, Martin focused on the numbing memories of what had brought him here in the first instance.

Steven had told him that he had been selected as the next "cloak", a term used by his employers meaning undercover operative. Such an appointment was considered an honour in this, the largest and best-hidden investigative agency in the country. Only those having real potential within the organization were given the chance to have a "cloak" assignment on his or her resumé.

Painfully gathered intelligence had warned of new waves of "people trafficking" along the eastern shipping corridors. All indicators pointed to a new yet powerful organization supplying illegal, under-skilled manpower from the east.

Much had been identified and understood about the carrier bringing these desperate souls into the country, yet, nothing was known about how they were being brought in, why or by whom.

Other, more senior and experienced colleagues were already out in the field, working on the project. Martin's brief had been simple.

He was to fly abroad to the main source of where the manpower was known to be recruited from, and, using false identities provided, ensure he was signed up to re-enter his own country in the illegal manner in which his fellow recruits would be exposed to. He was to capture as much evidence as he could, using the supplied high tech camera and recording devices, ensuring they were concealed at all times.

Colleagues would be waiting for him at his journey's end. Martin was to be the "mirror man", providing a visual and indisputable representation of the crimes committed once the perpetrators were brought to justice.

Initially, the operation had been simple in its execution. As planned, after extensive research and travelling that took over ten weeks, he was recruited on a street corner of a foreign city.

Once he had signed an unofficial document, he was marched away by two burly men, and literally thrown into the back of an articulated lorry, alone and confused. During the next seven hours, he was joined by many others, all men, until it was so cramped, no one could move without causing a chain reaction of added shuffling and hunching.

In stifling conditions, they were driven non-stop for the next sixteen hours, without food or water, until one hour ago; the drone of the lorry's engine was abruptly cut, its noise replaced by muffled shouting, hydraulic crashes, and the frenzied screaming of hungry seagulls.

Martin knew they had reached a ferry dock. Ever so slowly, the lorry was driven on, and, once the driver had exited the loading bay, this cargo of human desperation was alone.

If he survived whatever was left of this journey, he knew the outrage caused by his visual evidence would be enormous, forever his work.

As a tortured groan rang out through the dark trailer hold, Martin ruefully recalled Steven's parting philosophical words:

'You may want to cry for mercy when you think you've lost your way ...'

He remained silent. Inside, he laughed out loud.

# *Shy*

His head was pounding and his lungs felt as if they were on fire but he knew that he just could not afford to slow down. There was just too much at stake.

Simply walking the short hallway, leading to the front door was taking its physical toll on Richard. His joints screeched their displeasure as he continued ignoring the cramps in his sides, gulping for large mouthfuls of air instead.

Stopping was not an option. As he continued his tortuous journey inch by inch, the physical pain absorbing every pore of his body was indescribable. Adrenalin, the urgency of the situation and the demons that scourged his mind enabled him to continue.

For the third time, the urgent thumping at the thick wooden door froze his blood.

'I'm coming,' he gasped, leaning against the wall as he continued forwards. Beads of sweat from the sheer exertion of his efforts coursed from his forehead, pooling into his eyes, burning deep into his line of sight. The stinging pain was nothing compared to the pure terror enveloping him as he reached the point of no return.

Focusing on the ancient family portrait that hung directly opposite, he nervously inched his way ever closer to the door, ensuring he did not look down.

Barely a foot away, the muted banging from the other side once again made Richard's heart leap ever higher within his ribcage. Muffled voices penetrated the solid oak, causing him to lose balance. His reflex rebalancing movement prevented him from falling over, but did cause him to force his gaze towards the floor.

Despite the pure terror this alien voice had provoked, the sight at his feet galvanised him, and, wracked with a physical and emotional pain impossible to articulate, Richard lunged at the door with a final desperate move.

In the split second it took for him to reach the latch to meet the outsiders, as was sadly normal when he felt out of control, his life flashed before him.

Once again the traumatic image of his father leaving the family home forever haunted him. He was only six years old, and felt the shattering sensation of isolation thereafter. He saw himself sitting in the corner of his bedroom blaming himself night after night, cursing himself to a lifetime of loneliness as he did so.

Breath coming in ragged, sharp tearing rasps, Richard grabbed the door latch. Closing his eyes to compose himself, he mentally replayed the final pieces of his life's jigsaw, knowing that everything would change following this one heart-stopping moment.

At school, his teachers became concerned at how introverted he became in the months following his father's departure. His mother put it down to shyness, yet, for Richard, his life had become a maelstrom of anxiety. It bore into him like a searchlight; there was no avoiding it. Sweaty hands, pumping heart, churning stomach, dry mouth; shivering and a terror of losing control of his senses had become his way of existence.

Through the following years of adolescence and adulthood, his state of mind worsened. At sixteen, he had his first panic attack, his final exams being the trigger. By now, his mother had reluctantly accepted there may be a problem with her chronically shy, friendless son, and finally sought medical help.

On the day after his seventeenth birthday, he learnt he was not actually shy, but was suffering from acute Social Phobia – a fear of people. Over the next twelve months he learned to articulate how crippling his illness was, yet remained uncured.

Most people experienced Richard as painfully shy, and least now he was able to explain what the severity of his shyness meant; to shrink back from life itself – a weakening of the bonds of human connection.

In his twenty-second year one final, shattering experience sent him plummeting into the depths he had lived and experienced ever since.

Monica was the only attempt at a relationship he ever made. To this day, he still regretted attempting to explain how his mind worked:

'It's like being grabbed by an invisible assailant,' he tried to reason. 'You think you're losing your mind. It's horrible. You feel like a rabbit caught in the headlights, and your mind is always on a high state of alert.'

He had never seen her again after that revelation.

Since then, mother had taken care of everything. He never left the small terraced house they shared. His only life experiences had been through the Internet. Until today, even the friendliest knock on the front door would paralyse him with fear.

Opening his eyes, taking in the sight of his stricken elderly mother at the foot of the stairs, he opened the door, allowing the ambulance crew in, his first face-to-face contact with a human being for twenty years.

## *Fear of Flying*

Lee's bags were packed. He was ready for a fresh start in the States. All he hoped now was that those dreaded phone calls would stop. Was he now about to escape his stalker after all?

Sinking into the plush, comforting upholstery of his seat in the business class section of the New York bound 747, an audible sigh of relief escaped his lips, circulating around the steadily filling cabin. He closed his eyes. The soothing cacophony around him relaxed his mind, allowing uninvited memories to invade.

He snapped his eyes open, sitting bolt upright in the process. As his breathing quickened, he took in the activities around him, paying particular attention to the facial features of his transatlantic companions.

For too long, his mind had been hounded into a fortress of mistrust and suspicion. Until he was in the air and embarking on his new life, Lee would not let his defences slip. His sanity and wellbeing were at stake – the price of complacency too high.

Finally, the calm, confident tones of the captain broke through the busy chatter of occupants, informing them all of the essential flight details. As a perpetually smiling steward sealed the passenger door, he was past the point of no return. Everything he existed for was within his bags in the cargo hold, or his mind's eye.

Settling back in his seat again, taking little notice of the cabin crew's safety demonstration, the vast aircraft reversed inch by inch away from the boarding gate, towards the taxi point onto the main runway.

Taking one final glance around at the other passengers he closed his eyes. To the untrained, he resembled one more anxious passenger at take off. Reaching the taxi point at the end of the runway, the aircraft engaged forward thrust as Lee immersed himself in the events that had led to this moment.

As a highly competent, well respected GP in a large urban community, he was used to coming into contact with strangers daily. As his designated detective had reminded him, 'It could happen to anyone in your position.'

That was what made it so frightening. One day he was living his uncomplicated life, the next he was looking over his shoulder.

Initially, his problems began one evening when twenty text messages appeared on his mobile, all from an unrecognised number, stating their undying love for him with the words:

'Your voice comforts me beyond the stars. I will love you to all eternity.'

Ignoring them as a friend playing tricks, Lee took greater notice when the first calls arrived at home one week later.

Initially, they were the usual crank calls widely spoken of in his profession – mute with sounds of traffic or railway station announcements echoing eerily in the background. However, these calls were usually intercepted by the practice receptionists. How had his secure private number been breached?

After one week of up to five calls per evening like this, the caller – a female – finally broke her silence, threatening to kill him. His blood froze when she also reeled off the addresses of his nearest family. Whoever she was, she was well researched.

When informing the police, Lee unlocked a chain of events so frightening; his case was reported in the local press as, 'The most spine chilling example of a life under siege in this city ever.'

The calls continued – from phone boxes so that they were untraceable.

One evening, he came home from work to find every light in the house switched on. The next, he was awoken by the suffocating odour of gas, caused by a leaking hob. Had she come in and switched it on? Was she watching him as he ran from the house in terror? The fear and uncertainty went on for weeks.

Finally, when his mother and sister began receiving calls from the same woman, the police arranged the "sting" operations that ultimately lead to her capture.

Paying a weekend visit to his mother, teams of police waited at strategic points to intercept every telephone box in the area on the Saturday morning. As the calls came, for most of the morning, they missed her, but then, just after midday, she was finally apprehended.

She was identified as Maria Quarry, a relatively new patient of Lee, only registering six months ago, having been wrongly diagnosed with clinical depression by her previous GP.

For Lee, the damage was irreparable. Despite her capture and incarceration pending trial, escaping the mental prison Quarry had cursed upon him was impossible.

Leaving was the only option. America would provide his salvation.

As the screaming engines catapulted the massive aircraft skywards, the gentle tap on his shoulder brought him around.

'Hello Doctor,' Maria's unmistakeable voice whispered gently in his ear. 'I've been looking for you everywhere ...'

# *A Timely Penance*

An aggressive knock at the door was all that announced the arrival into Jason's life of something truly horrific. Opening the door, he looked down to find a cardboard box. And it was ticking.

Prickles of fresh autumn air caressed his face as he saw the hunched figure, back turned to him, exiting the property, onto the deserted street beyond the boundary of his garden. The shadowed figure was indistinguishable in the evening twilight.

'Wait!' Jason shouted, running in bare feet towards the delivery man. Even though it was just after seven, the chill in the air was noticeable. Having only just returned home from another busy day in the office, he was in a state of half undress, and had not thought about this before answering the door. The shards of pain shooting into the soles of his feet were acting as an obvious reminder to him now.

Reaching the point where his garden became part of the quiet suburban cul-de-sac, he was astounded that the figure was nowhere to be seen. Left, right, front and back, the person had gone, as if swallowed up by the onset of darkness.

As his heartbeat continued to rise in a crescendo of anxiety, he carefully made his way back to the front door. His wife, Annette, had come to investigate the source of disruption. She too had only just returned home from work, and was agitated at the violation of her shared down time with her husband.

'Who was that?' she enquired, 'and more importantly, *what* is *that?*' she demanded, urgently, pointing at the large brown box. He noticed that the ticking was getting louder.

Despite his physical symptoms of confusion, his mind spoke to him in practical tones.

'Not sure. I think it was a delivery man who had to wait around for someone to come back to the house,' he mused, trying to retain a grip on logic, even though he hadn't looked at his parcel yet.

'Did he get a signature to prove late delivery?' she asked accusingly, an edge of apprehension creeping into her voice. 'What sort of delivery man would lie in wait for someone to get home?' she thought aloud, her suspicion audibly rising.

Turning her stare back to him, she stiffened.

'Well ... did you get a signature or proof of identity? Because I think that this is just a little too weird Jason.'

'No,' Jason honestly replied, picking up the empty box, again noticing the ticking noise was quickening once more. As he bent to straighten himself up, his lower back creaked in protest at the sudden movement – a sensation he'd never felt before.

Placing the package on the floor in his hallway, it occured to him that his actions verged on the suicidal.

'What are you doing?' Annette screeched, running to the back of the house as she continued to protest. 'It could be a bomb for all you know!'

'It could, but I know it's not!' he barked defensively.

'How could you know that?' she moaned, her slow shuffling steps indicating that she was moving back towards her husband, possibly realising that maybe there was not a bomb.

He didn't have the heart to tell her the truth. He couldn't recall the last time he felt so frightened. He was staring aghast at the addressee label that sat proudly on top of the package. It was inscribed with the words 'Jason – Older' in thick, scraggy handwriting.

'Gypsy,' he whispered under his breath.

'Jason, oh my God! Your hair!' Annette had sidled up to him, suddenly becoming hysterical, experiencing emotions that transcended anything beyond normal fear or concern in a human.

He knew what was happening. His hips suddenly ached as he painfully shuffled to the full-length mirror at the end of the hallway. Upon reaching it, he was met with a reflection he did not even know or recognize, such was the sudden effect of the contents of the box.

What was once a thick mane of black hair had turned into a wispy, pure white tangled mess. Wrinkles formed in the corners of his eyes as he stood there, painfully mesmerised by his metamorphosis.

Behind him, Annette blacked out, hitting the ground with a heavy thud. It was probably for the best – at least she wouldn't have to see the end. In the background, the box ticked ever louder, even faster.

As his spine gave way to the ravages of time, forcing him to stoop, he knew there were only minutes left. Old age continued ravaging his body and mind, just as the gypsy had promised. Raising his head, he took one last look at himself. In the place of a fit and healthy twenty-seven year old young man, stood a withered, sunken, aged being on the verge of extinction.

He recalled the small, tatty street boy he had encountered in the busy city centre street that morning. He vividly saw himself forcefully push the troubled youngster to the ground in answer to his request for 'a few pennies for my family.'

Falling to his knees, he remembered shouting at the child as he lay on the cold concrete floor: 'I don't have *time* for this – tell your parents to get a job!'

Finally, he recalled himself jumping back at the appearance of a man – presumably the boy's father – stopping him dead in his tracks, only several yards further along the same street. Pointing directly at Jason's forehead, he growled a menacing, rhythmic monotone.

'From now, time will be an issue no more. Pity the man to suffer the ravages, for time bringeth all existence to an end prematurely …' Then he was gone.

Brushing himself down, Jason made nothing of the situation, and continued on his journey. If only he had known. If only he had believed – or apologised …

As he collapsed, passing through the bonds of this earthly existence, inside the box the ticking stopped.

# *Family Secrets*

She froze, both hands on the lid of the box, unable to wrench her trembling hands away, but terrified of what she might find if she gave into temptation. No. She had to know. Slowly, she lifted the lid.

Its aged hinges creaked as Emma frantically blinked, fighting back stinging tears that blinded her visually and emotionally. Now fully open, the wooden lid was agape, revealing its dark contents.

However, such was the torrent of panic gripping her, as the tears flowed uncontrollably, it was impossible to actually see the life-changing secrets. Snapping the box closed again, she carefully placed it on her marital bed and lurched into the adjoining bathroom.

Dabbing at sore, tired eyes, Emma fought to control her inner turmoil, sucking in large rasping gulps of air, desperately trying to rationalise her actions and emotions to the small object – the *thing* – sitting on their bed. The glare of the small sodium light above the vanity mirror bit into her rawness. Lowering her stare, for the thousandth time, she replayed the telephone call that her brought her to this place of anguish, hurt and deceit.

At the exact moment the shrill, penetrating ringing of the phone broke the silent house, Emma was disposing of what remained of breakfast's leftovers. Stephen, her husband of sixteen years had ambled out of the house to work in exactly the same manner as always, and their two daughters had been safely deposited at school.

Upon answering, she was greeted by the sombre tones of her sister-in-law, Marian. Despite never having the best of relationships with her, Emma was immediately relieved it was a family member, and not the school or Stephen's office relaying an emergency or crisis.

However, her relief would evaporate within seconds.

Coldly and calmly, Marion informed her of the shattering revelation about Stephen that had been 'kept a secret for long enough.' The words that were to change her life forever were expressed cruelly in their directness. Furthermore, Marion was able to tell her exactly where to locate the proof to support her allegation.

Before Emma was able to ask questions, her sister-in-law hung up.

Standing numb in the hallway, Emma shook herself down, disbelieving at what she had heard. Why on earth would Stephens's sister say something so malicious and cruel about her own brother? It did not make sense, they had both been close for as long as she could remember.

Despite wishing to dismiss the conversation from her mind, Emma found herself irresistibly drawn to the garage, and in particular, Stephen's golf club bag.

According to Marion, she would find the object – a small battered mahogany cigar box – in the side pocket of the luxury leather club carrier.

Not wanting to believe that she would be so suspicious after such a cruel accusation against her husband – especially after who it had come from – Emma's blood froze as she removed the small, hand carved box from the exact place Marion had described.

Incredulous in her deep shock, Emma moved back into the bedroom, gingerly holding the object with its contents of potentially shattering secrets as if it were red hot, burning into her very soul.

Breathing now restored to normal, eyes swollen and sore from the tears of realization, Emma returned to her bed, perched onto the edge, and in one sudden movement, tore the lid from its timeworn anchor point.

The letter at the top of the small pile of faintly scented papers was handwritten, unprotected by an envelope. She gently removed it, fighting an inner rage to simply tear it into little pieces – as much as it tormented her, she had to read it, she had to validate everything with her own eyes. Very carefully, and very slowly, she began to read:

'My dearest, darling Stephen ...'

After reading the first paragraph, she had captured everything she needed to know. Skipping to the end of the second handwritten sheet, the signature confirmed everything. His infidelities were undeniable, his betrayal beyond forgiveness.

For several seconds, the room around her spun, but, as she once again fought to regain control of her emotions; the sound of Stephen's car outside returned her to her senses.

Making no attempt to return the box to its original hiding place, Emma allowed the letter to gently fall from her hand. It floated to the floor in small, rhythmic arcing movements, as she hurled the remaining letters across the entire span of their bed.

Lying face down on her pillow, she heard him breathlessly enter the room.

'We need to talk ...' he blurted, panicked and agitated.

His timing was perfect. After all, it's not often a wife is betrayed by her philandering husband for the love and affection of another man – especially if the other man is your own brother.

## *Tanglewood*

Paralysed with terror, he froze, breath held, eyes bulging, desperately waiting for the footsteps to pass, and praying his hiding place would conceal him. As the footsteps drew nearer, his panic intensified.

Lucid thoughts gave way to terror shrouding him like a dark cloak, and David Bennett mentally cursed himself for coming into the woods alone, with no means of contact to the outside world, having left his mobile in the glove compartment of his car – safely parked far away from this place.

Fighting the urge to jump from behind the hollow oak tree he desperately hoped shielded him, the audible proximity of his fellow visitor – or was it dweller? – drew ever closer, so much so, he was sure he could faintly hear the rhythmic whisper of its breathing.

Hunching as low as creaking joints allowed, David knew he was being hunted. What he had just seen and felt confirmed everything, and, if he managed to get out of here in one piece, his findings would do nothing to put the village at rest whatsoever.

He had been brought to Smokeham Woods at the request of the village police officer, who, as a last resort, had been urged to engage the services of a paranormal investigator by frightened residents, whose everyday calm in this tranquil backwater had been shattered by a series of unexplained, distressing events over the last two months.

Without warning, strange things had been afflicted upon those who entered a hitherto well-used part of the wood known as 'The Brambles.' Suddenly, it had become a place of fear and foreboding.

Dogs had inexplicably disappeared whilst being walked, only yards from their unsuspecting owners. Reports of strange smells from the ground, and lights in the sky bombarded the police switchboard daily. Finally, reinforcements were called in, and a manhunt initiated with the disappearance of the Reverend Nigel Groate, the vicar of Smokeham. He had not been heard or seen for seven days, his route the morning he disappeared almost certainly taking in 'The Brambles'.

Despite an exhaustive search of the entire area, the whereabouts of the vicar were still unknown.

For all his extensive experience in paranormal activity, and despite the clamour for answers, David felt there was a rational answer for the occurrences, and, this evening, had started work with an entirely open mind in search of a logical answer.

Entering an investigation scene by cover of night was his usual modus operandi. Walking calmly into Smokeham Woods, his first thought was of the church on the hill above the village. It stood as if protecting the parishioners from the dark woods beyond, yet forlorn at the loss of its inhabitant.

He felt the strange atmosphere of the woods immediately. Stunted trees twisted and writhed as if in pain. Thick bracken swirled, whispering a sinister invitation in the gentle breeze. Within one hundred yards, he came across a large crater, its origin uncertain, yet it was clear that nothing grew within – the barren soil was parched, all life taken extinguished.

Stopping to relay his thoughts into a small dictaphone, for no apparent reason, he suddenly felt faint. It was if he had been submerged beneath a wave of fatigue. Moving several steps forwards, a searing pain pierced deep into his skull, as if his eardrums were being pulled from the inside out.

Throughout the sudden change to his physical state, curiosity kept hold over him, and, when he had walked a further fifty yards, the painful effects disappeared simultaneously.

As his heartbeat rose rapidly, he could see or feel no other presence with him – strangely, all he felt was an eerie silence.

Finally, upon reaching 'The Brambles', Bennett was confronted by something he could never have prepared himself for.

A dark shape, unmoving, about twelve feet tall; whilst not distinctive in outline, he knew it definitely wasn't smoke or a bush, the only description that came to him was "black mass". As quickly as it appeared, it was gone before his very eyes.

Rushing to where it had stood, he looked to the grassy, mud-caked ground, searching for some evidence of a solid shape or imprint to back up what he thought he had witnessed. At the very spot where the form had appeared, he came upon the clear imprint of a four clawed foot – twice the width of humans, yet very narrow at the heel.

Suddenly, he felt cold – very cold, then, came the footsteps.

Instinctively, David Bennett had run for cover to the nearest place that would conceal him. Now, as tears of panic and fear rolled down his cheeks, he knew that he had made a terrible mistake.

Illuminating the gloom, two sharp yellow eyes, inhuman, soulless and sightless met his.

Passing out in fear, Bennett's last visual memory was of the missing vicar, a man whose photograph he had never previously seen.

# *Meltdown*

Friday, 6.00 am.The sun rose from its hidden southerly domain, lazily touching the rim of a crystal blue early August sky, weather announcer excitedly informing the waking world of staggering news.

'Today's the day folks!' he boldly declared. '100 degree temperatures are expected across the county, make sure you apply the sun block, and get the cold beers in!' For good measure, he signed off with a sickeningly cheery, 'Have a *great* day!'

Sat in a gridlocked queue, temperatures outside already nudging 85, all access roads to the international airport's gleaming terminal building blocked, Mark Warren cursed under his breath.

Having sat motionless in this simmering tangle of overheating metal and driver temperaments for nearly an hour, he wondered if fate was in the process of playing a cruel trick, thwarting what little ambition was left inside him.

In front, the two occupants of a blue saloon were in the throes of a serious altercation, judging by the wild waving of arms, pointing and, rocking of their vehicle.

As an experienced daily commuter, Mark's insider knowledge knew only too well that the summer schedule early morning low-cost flights were well under way, delivering their human cargoes – affectionately known as the 'bucket and spade brigade' – to every part of continental Europe.

Each carrier had appointed "slots" for take off, with ever tightening turn around "windows" – 'A plane isn't making money when it's idle on the ground, sir' – (a hard nosed airline pilot had once told Mark during a complimentary "meet the management" PR exercise), so, prepaid passengers, missing or not – take off times were stuck to, yield numbers were met, and, if lucky, all your passengers would be on board.

Ignoring his in-car clock, Mark flicked his wrist, taking the time from his basic wristwatch, received as an eighth birthday present. 6.15, yet no movement, not even an inch. He turned the screeching radio off with a frustrated snap. He only had to look in front of him to know that that approach road was rammed solid. Some idiot, now excitedly blaring that, "It was best to avoid at all costs – find an alternative route" did not help, especially as the fool wasn't even making any effort to describe what was *causing* the problem, or *how long it would take to clear.*

Congestion problems were a daily battle at this time of year. Realizing his own chances of making his meeting on time were slipping away by the second, Mark was hard-pressed to remember a time when the approach road was *this* bad.

Despite the air conditioning blasting at full power, tiny beads of sweat formed on his upper lip. Temperatures were rising fast and not just those in the atmosphere.

Winding his window down for added relief, the noise of the outside world was missing something. Mark could clearly hear the sizzling of overheating engines upfront, but no running ones. This was bad. Whatever was causing the bottleneck up front, the message had come down for drivers to turn their engines off.

'We're in it for the duration then. Great!' Mark bashed the leather steering wheel in desperate frustration.

Commuting 500 miles to work on a fully expensed city hopper was always an adventure, never more so during the peak holiday season, where his daily travelling routine was supplemented with an additional 5000 sun seeking companions.

When he started the job, the airport was a small operation, convenient, well run and a fantastic alternative to the huge, sprawling affairs in the capital city. Due to the educational needs of his autistic son, and a desire to keep his marriage alive, it came with relief that the Company were prepared to pay for and put up with such a daily commute. It was also "doable", as long as the ludicrously early morning starts could be maintained.

However, the last eighteen months were a time of great change for the airport, the City, and its citizens. Due to lower rents, two major low-cost airlines had moved from the capital, and set up their main "hubs" here. This had opened up several dozen bargain routes, previously unheard of, unavailable in this locality. With it came expansion and new employment opportunities.

The response was overwhelming. Thousands of bright-eyed travellers descended on the revamped, extended airport, from conurbations across the whole region, enraptured by the notion of not having to make the arduous trek to the capital.

6.30. Still no movement. Several motorists were out of their cars, stretching and yawning.

Some (he recognised them as fellow business travellers) spoke on mobile phones, others slumped on their vehicles, heads in hands, early days of their holidays going up in smoke. Directly in front, Mark now clearly heard screams of abuse being hurled venomously between driver and co-driver, the use of language matching their silhouetted gestures in perfect synchronicity. The temperature gauge read 89 Fahrenheit.

Concerns began circulating at the super growth of the airport last October. Summer schedules completed, in a triumphant press conference, record passenger numbers, yields and local employment figures were announced. The local economy prospered, and everyone had aeroplanes to thank. During the same announcement, an unsuspecting public was informed that a series of daily long haul flights, by the *world's* premium airline, would commence in August, heightening further global awareness of the city.

7.00 am. Replaying that press conference mentally, Mark smiled. He too, had stepped from his car, phoned the head of recruitment, informing him to cancel their appointment. The irony was not lost on either of them during that call. Quite simply, their business would have to wait. Around him, several hundred weary, angst ridden travellers spread out among the grass verges, framing the main road. Many of them, having set out picnic blankets and towels, diligently applied sun protection, starting their summer holidays there and then. Mark chuckled to himself, running a hand through his perspiration soaked black hair. The argument within the car before him raged. Unbeknown to him, the city was beginning to fall to its knees.

Thundering overhead, screaming jets took off and landed every few minutes. Those setting off were now likely to be half full, and the elongated snake of stationary traffic would be reaching the city centre, blocking all artery roads, suffocating life from the day before it began. As the temperature outside hit 95, things were hotter in the thousands of stranded cars, rupturing access points across every key intersection in the city.

Seventeen miles from the city centre, Mark took a keen interest as developments in front became more worrying. Clearly emanating from the blue car, the series of expletives and threats had become so graphic, *hate driven* and real, several of those stood by now gathered with Mark aside his car, discussing the best way to resolve their little crisis. Of particular concern, the two protagonists were male and female, and sinisterly, violent threats came from the man. Despite this, neither had made any effort to wind their windows up, to shut the world out.

'Where's a policeman when you need one?' a male holidaymaker, resplendent in a garish orange beach shirt moaned.

'Probably stuck in this lot too!' he answered himself, laughing aloud. Others saw the funny side, joining in, but not all. Mark was only too aware that the police were going to have more than a mere traffic jam to worry about if things could not be sorted quickly. One of their newly formed group, a commuter Mark knew as Graham, had heard on radio the city was a clogged-up mess, ring roads and all three surrounding motorways backing up also.

This was what it was all about twelve months ago – news – making it for all the right reasons. Once the increased flights roster was announced, initial reaction was celebratory. Then questions came. How would the city cope? It had only just 'gotten away with it' this year.

The questions were valid. For, despite the accelerated status of the airport as one of the world's fastest growing, it could not keep up. An already creaking infrastructure would not cope under the additional strain. No motorway links existed nearby. The nearest railway station was City Centre. Coach and bus links only ran fourteen hours a day, causing additional congestion during "quieter" times. Critics had a field day. 'Our airport has got too big for its and our own good!' they cried. 'It's only a matter of time, and the greatest transportation disaster in history will bring ridicule and shame upon us!'

'And so you have been proven correct, my friends,' Mark hissed through gritted teeth, those words ringing in his ears.

Suddenly, a petite, bikini clad viciously angry blonde jumped from the driver's side of the blue saloon, stomping furiously to the passenger door, screaming and shouting, totally enraged. In her right hand, a Swiss army knife, poised and drawn to inflict damage. Ripping the door open, she reached inside with her left arm, forcefully pulling out her male companion by his long brown hair. As he howled in pain, the blonde pushed him against the side of the car, forcing him to stand fully upright before her. Holding the knife above her head to his throat, her enraged threats to, 'Kill him dead right now,' were deadly serious.

Mark, with his small band of stranded kinsmen acted swiftly. As one, they pulled back the small female, rescuing her considerably bigger husband, avoiding a major incident to further the torment of the moment. When tempers eventually cooled, the argument's source, trivial in its content, was explosive in its outcome. Quite simply, the young husband had the gall to suggest that waiting in the queue would have been avoided had he been driving.

As he sat on the grass verge, lunching with the Younis family, who had been due to fly to Athens at 6.30 – seven hours ago – Mark contemplated how to manage his future following today's debacle.

Vehicles would start moving in two hours. He knew this morning's blockage was caused by "sheer weight of traffic" and the "minor" complication of a fractured gas main, underneath the main airport car park, taking all day to fix. Additionally, word of mouth and the frenzied radio reports had told, that, as a result of the city wide gridlock, the whole social structure collapsed, resulting in, amongst other things, three separate incidents of attempted murder, fuelled by excessive heat and road rage.

It had been quite a day. Mark made up his mind. Tomorrow, he would again phone the interview panel chairman, withdrawing immediately. Next, contact his employer, tendering his resignation. His situation was untenable. His position as development director for the airport authority now unthinkable, and his application for MD of the airport itself, quite frankly, was not important any more.

## *Doppelganger*

When I first appeared, the hearts and minds of the genteel folk of the village square scurrying about their business must have received something of a sudden shock.

'You appeared naked – totally stark naked – from out of nowhere, in broad daylight, and then started running up and down the green! What do you mean, you have never been to this place in your life?'

Detective Chief Inspector Sidney Owen was at his wits' end with me. As I sat forlorn and alone in the interview room, I was at a loss for words, paralysed by shock and panic.

'Look at the CCTV pictures! The best quality money can buy! There's no mistake, it's you isn't it Mr Sadler?'

There was no denying it. The A4 high definition prints sitting upon the Formica desk were of me. As naked as the day I was born, clearly running and jumping through the packed village square.

'Well, yes … I mean … but it can't be …' I groaned, 'I swear, I've never been there in my life – I don't even know where in the country Upton Nimbly is!'

My court appointed solicitor rolled his eyes. The last thing he wanted was a lunatic to waste taxpayers' money on trying to defend.

Slumping in my chair, my sense of reality was slipping away from me. It had been three hours since I had been awoken by the sound of frantic banging at my front door. Bleary-eyed from sleep, I was confronted by two police officers, who when confirming who I was, requested my assistance in answering some questions 'down at the station' in relation to an incident last week at a village in the North I had never even heard of.

Wishing to co-operate fully, I duly obliged, and now find myself looking at these pictures, which are categorically clear – me in my full glory, sharing it with the rest of the population of Upton Nimbly.

'Maybe you can also explain your other disturbing appearances over the last two weeks Mr Sadler?'

I was brought out of my trance by the policeman's harsh tones.

'You mean there's more?' I spluttered, genuinely frightened now.

'Oh yes, there's more. Why don't you stop mucking us all around, and admit to all of them?'

'Admit to what?' Panic gripped my heart with its suffocating icy tentacles. The dark grey windowless walls of the small interrogation room were suffocating me, I had no idea what to do or say.

Sighing heavily, DCI Owen pulled a folder from his briefcase, slowly, deliberately, and just a little too dramatically.

'OK. If you want to play it like this, let's share everything we have on you ... I have to say Mr Sadler, your high jinks have made you something of a celebrity up and down the country.'

Grinning savagely, he pulled many more images of me compromised and unclothed, spreading them all across the desk as he did so. In swift succession, he identified the dates, times and locations of each one, jabbing a podgy finger at each one to emphasise the heinous nature of my crimes.

'This was last Tuesday, midday, Binting High Street ... Wednesday, 3 pm, Plifney Shopping Centre ...'

And so he went on, another eleven times. It was torture. For each one, I had no idea how I had got to those unfamiliar places, let alone be accountable for my actions. It was truly terrifying. And yet, there I was, my features unmistakeable to the finest detail, causing untold distress to men, women and children going about their daily business.

Yet, there was something even more disturbing about those pictures, way beyond the acts themselves or my complete amnesia to committing them. It was my face, or rather, the complete lack of expression on it in every single picture.

Instead of mad, lunatic eyes boring from the images, with contorted smiles of chaos demonstrating that I knew what I was doing, there was nothing. I looked washed out and pale, almost hypnotised. I appeared to have little regard for the world around me. Equally, my visual appearance demonstrated a complete regard for my own welfare and wellbeing. Equally unsettling for me was the fact that, considering we were experiencing one of the coldest Decembers on record, I did not appear to be remotely affected by the biting sub-zero temperatures that were bringing the rest of the country to a gradual standstill.

'How could I have been in all of these places in only a week?' I asked, thinking aloud.

'I'm the one asking the questions Mr Sadler – I will kindly remind you to respect that!' he haughtily rebuffed.

‘How could I have got to all those places? I can’t even drive …’ Wrapped in thought, asking more questions to a highly antagonised police officer, I was inadvertently making my situation far worse by the second.

Just as the DCI looked as if he may explode in exasperation, a new voice stepped in to pull all of us back from the brink.

Up to this point, my court appointed solicitor, Mayweather Jackson esq. had been ominously silent. Despite his grand name, he was a small, ferrety-looking man, dressed in a crumpled beige suit with a pink shirt that had not seen an iron for at least three months, and a brown tie with orange stripes that proudly displayed a crusty old egg stain. When I shook his clammy hand fifteen minutes earlier, he simply said, ‘Call me Jacko – everyone else does,’ in a reedy nasal monotone.

‘I would like a minute with my client alone if you please Detective Chief Inspector,’ he whinnied, clasping his hands together in mock prayer.

‘Very well,’ DCI Owen hissed, ‘one minute. But nothing funny – we will be watching.’ He jerked his thumb towards the small viewing panel on the cold, forbidding steel door of the interrogation room. I think he was probably grateful to get away from the odd-looking, slightly repulsive legal guardian.

The interrogator and his hitherto silent, almost comatose sidekick, Sergeant something or other, both left the room with plenty of scuffing of chairs and a dramatic slow walk to the door. They obviously wanted a quick resolution to this job, and my complete lack of mental cohesion was beginning to wear them down. I was the last thing they needed to worry about three days before Christmas.

As the door slammed shut with an alarming, foreboding echo, Jacko urgently swivelled in his chair, and grabbed my chin in his left hand, forcing me to look him in the eye. His body language and verbal delivery had completely transformed. No longer did he look like a washed-up pathetic rodent, he was more a lion, and I was infringing on his domain.

'Now, you are going to tell me the truth, because right now, I can't help you unless you give me an idea about what's going on. These men are looking to close this one down, and, at the moment, it looks like you will be spending Christmas staring at the walls of a prison cell. The only thing you will have to look forward to will be your hearing in the New Year. Do you understand?' he hissed, with urgency reflected in his blazing eyes.

'Yes,' I gibbered.

'Then let's try to make sense of this … These pictures, are they definitely you?'

'Looks that way,' I retorted sulkily.

'That's no help,' he barked. 'Do you have a twin? Are you on medication for deluded tendencies? Do you have any alibis for the times in question?'

'No to all three,' I moaned, feeling more and more desperate by the second. I live alone, and prefer it that way. For the whole week, I had spent no time in any one else's company.

'Then the only thing we can do is accept the charge, and if no bail is offered, I will have to work up an insanity plea for your hearing in the New Year.'

'But I'm not insane!' I stood up as I yelled, forcing a uniformed officer to come rushing into the room, most likely in the belief that I was just about to cause some harm to my lawyer.

'I'm perfectly in control of my mind!' I finished, as I was screamed at to, 'Sit down and stay still!' by our new companion.

'Really officer, it's OK.' Jacko smiled, unperturbed by my little outburst.

Turning his stare back to me, he finished our conversation with a brutal and telling statement. 'Are you sure? Because if you can't remember something that may help in the next two minutes, you are going to be charged, and Santa does not visit people detained at her majesty's leisure.'

I was at a complete loss for words. My mind was numb, my spirit shattered. I had done nothing wrong. That person blankly staring out from those pictures – he wasn't me. However, due to the overwhelming evidence stacked against me, I was beginning to wonder if my fractured mind was playing tricks on me, if I really *had* done these things I was accused of, and I had subconsciously repressed them.

Sitting motionless, feeling sorry for myself, the room had become alarmingly quiet. Even the uniformed officer seemed to be a little agitated by the lack of activity between me and my lawyer. As the seconds slowly passed, all that could be heard was the rhythmic pattern of my breathing.

'Strange ...' Jacko muttered into his cupped hand, 'they've been gone for fifteen minutes now.'

Had that amount of time really passed?

Suddenly, as if prompted by Jacko's statement, the door crunched open with great force, and DCI Owen re-entered the room. His features were pale and drawn, yet at the same time, he looked furious and bewildered in equal measures.

Slumping in the chair directly opposite me, he ordered the uniform to leave the room. I could see he was gripping yet more images tightly in his clenched fist. My heart virtually stopped beating at the thought of even more damning, humiliating images of me.

'DCI, you for one should know that this is a breach of protocol to continue with an interview alone. I must advise you …'

'Advise me nothing Jacko!' he mumbled, reaching across to the tape recorder. However, instead of re-engaging it, he simply muttered the time and date into the machine, and, for the record, terminated the interview.

My confusion was crushing me. I could barely hear what was being said to me, my thoughts were now so incoherent. All I could do was look at the new pictures that had been neatly laid out on the table in front of me.

There were four of them in total, all with the same image, taken from different angles. I looked to Jacko, disbelieving. He returned my look with an equally incredulous stare.

'These pictures were taken thirty minutes ago, in Bradlington Flyover, thirty miles from here. First indications are that the time of the incident was 1 pm,' Owen droned, with more than a hint of disbelief – or was that defeat – in his voice.

'But we were in here at the time! That was only 1 hour ago!' I exclaimed, too frightened to think straight. 'We've been here since 9 am this morning!'

'This just can't be!' Jacko gasped. 'I mean, this is impossible ...'

He was not wrong either, for there before us, in full colour for all to see, were four pictures of a young man, totally naked, freshly deceased.

'Apparently, we have a credible witness who saw him jump from the flyover into the oncoming traffic below. She says that despite her frantic shouts to stop him, he just calmly climbed over the safety rail, as if in a trance, and over he went.'

Shock gripped what remained of my senses like a tightening vice. My mind was being ripped to pieces. My sense of reality was struggling to comprehend the sight that lay before me.

For there, right before my very eyes, despite the number of times I tried to rationalise, I was looking at four pictures of me. Naked. The suicidal jumper was a man who was the exact mirror image of me – I *was* the dead man. The only clue to his identity was sitting in the interrogation room, aghast, in complete shock. I had the most extreme alibi in the history of the criminal justice system. My last memory before passing out was of DCI Owen stating that I was free to go due to 'inconclusive evidence ...'

When I came round, I was laying in a hospital bed, my mother sitting upright in a chair beside me. In the corner of my private room, mounted on a wall bracket, a television was relaying the early evening news.

Ignoring the loving messages of relief and care from the woman who had brought me into the world, I strained to hear the TV. My picture filled the room. I was the main headline on this particular day, and as is appropriate in such times, Jacko had taken centre stage to grab his fifteen minutes of fame.

He looked slightly strained and bemused as his rodent-like visage swallowed the entire screen, yet as his words reached my ears, my spine tingled at the reality of the week's events, and his summarisation of what they meant:

'Ladies and Gentlemen, it is perhaps a telling symptom of modern society that some people can disappear and not be missed. Equally, there are dozens of accounts of people who have suddenly appeared, usually dead – sometimes in strange circumstances – without any identification on their person, and without family or friends searching for them. Sometimes the manner in which someone passes is so unusual, it is only a matter of time – beginning with our criminal investigative system – before we are forced to look at these matters with an alternative mindset. The time has come for change ...'

I laid back in the comfort of the hospital bed and closed my eyes. It was going to take some time before I would come to terms with the life and death of the "phantom" me, or of the impact he would have on the world.

# *Change of Heart*

Graham looked at his new-born child's face and went cold. He was the spitting image of his best friend.

There was absolutely no debating it. It was all there; piercing blue almond shaped eyes, a perfectly symmetrical nose, rounded at the tip, Cupid's bow lips that turned down at slightly different angles each side of the face, framed by perfectly round pink cheeks. Only the thick black matted hair of the infant provided any sort of differential to the obvious lines of parentage.

This in itself was hardly surprising, all things considered; however, a sudden overwhelming sense of clammy discomfort enveloped Graham's heart. The realisation slammed into him, thinly disguised as a wave of uncertainty and panic.

Still holding Sebastian (for this was the name given to the child several months ago, when the scan revealed the developing foetus was actually going to be a he), the newly anointed father immediately felt guilt that such a happy, joyous event could be tinged with feelings of doubt and uncertainty, betraying all that was discomforting about bringing a new life into the world under flawed circumstances.

'Is he OK? Is my baby OK?' gasped Helena, lying exhausted on the delivery bed, still breathless and flushed following the difficult fourteen hour labour.

Graham's veins filled with ice, heart freezing, each breath catching in his throat. Had she really just said that? The stilted look of panic he received from the corner of the room did little to relieve him of any concern.

'He's perfect, everything where it should be, all moving in the right direction!'

He quipped, trying to make light of the moral guilt trip that was creeping into his every pore. He could not bring himself to look at Helena in the eye yet, it was all he could do to keep hold of the infant as the ground started to move beneath his feet. Breathing a deep lungful of air, Graham was determined to avoid a very public panic attack, especially here of all places.

'Wonderful! Our precious angel has arrived!' Despite her exhaustion, Helena could barely contain her excitement. She tried to awkwardly sit herself upright in the bed, craning her neck to catch the first full visual memory of her son.

They had been on their own in the delivery room for the past twenty minutes, the two midwives, nurse and doctor satisfied their work was complete. It was now the precious window of time needed for mother and baby to spend time bonding, getting used to the sense of intimate connection, unbreakable for all eternity.

Every single second of those twenty minutes had become more and more awkward, as Graham's pronounced joy at the arrival of his first born became further tainted by the circumstances to which he had been brought into the world.

'Are *you* OK?' Helena asked anxiously, her breathing more rhythmic and controlled. She had given up trying to raise herself from the prone position in which she lay, instead concentrating on Graham, trying to relay to him a sense of calmness that he was obviously searching for.

Buying a precious few seconds before responding, he took the ten short steps needed to cross the delivery room in order to reach the window. Opening it, he was grateful for the cool, crisp late September air to caress his face, allowing him to marginally clear his senses. How he wished he were strolling out there in the perfectly manicured grounds right now!

'*I'm* fine. He's fine. It's just ...' His voice trailed off. Still cradling his new precious gift, his mind ran a rapid series of flashbacks, a moving picture show, detailing the chronological series of circumstances and events leading to this momentous occasion.

He recalled how they had been informed by the doctors that their longed-for child would only be gifted upon them with the assistance of science. How they had taken the doctors' advice, their lives full of hope and optimism as the treatment commenced, only for those dreams to be cruelly shattered by the failure of the very science the doctors had so placed their faith in. Not once, but twice. Feelings of utter despair and hopelessness marking the next turbulent period in their fifteen year marriage, a union stretched beyond breaking point time and time again by their desperation to add a new human being to the family line.

And then, just as all hope was to be abandoned by both of them, an unusual, unforeseen opportunity – their last chance of hope which must be taken. It was not without risks, but to be embraced in spite of this.

A small wry smile broke out on Graham's face as Sebastian slumbered peacefully in his arms. Looking out beyond the hospital grounds, he allowed himself the selfish luxury of reflection, with a little justification as to why they had reached this point.

Helena and Graham were inseparable throughout childhood, beyond the burgeoning onset of adolescence into young adulthood. Growing up as neighbours in the tougher part of their home town, theirs was a solid bond of friendship; having experienced the full spectrum of highs and lows, emotionally and physically, as all lifelong friendships invariably do.

Theirs was a strange union to many who did not understand the dynamics of their relationship. They were both comfortable in the knowledge they could never live without each other, yet fully understood it was impossible for them to exist as a romantically intertwined couple. From the age of fifteen, Helena had got to a specific point in her life where she understood that her sexual orientation was not to follow the more conventional direction of her peers.

In spite of the shattering disappointment to Graham, who to this day considered Helena to be the one true love of his life, their bond grew ever stronger as they embraced their newly developed attitudes on life together.

'It's absolutely the right thing to do!' Helena had exclaimed on that fateful night eighteen months ago.

Without warning, she had turned up on their doorstep, flowers in one hand for Stephanie, and a pocket full of dreams to be realised for them both. Despite remaining in weekly contact by telephone, their professional and personal lives had made it difficult for the two friends to spend any time together outside of Christmas or major family gatherings.

Once the euphoria of Helena's offer had sunk in, the rest of the evening was spent in deep and intense conversation as to her motives for the offer:

'Because I love you both – it's as simple as that – through to any potential emotional or physical catastrophes.'

'What if you change your mind?' Stephanie asked. 'I won't, trust me,' was the curt response.

After four hours and three bottles of wine of protracted debate, at the point where emotions were starting to run high, they all agreed to call it a night.

Pausing at the front door as she left, Helena turned to Graham, and, as a solitary tear defiantly ran down her left cheek, told him that, 'I came to help the man I love most in the world. Don't do this to us. Let it happen. I love you.' She abruptly turned and left, swallowed up by the sultry summer night.

After staying up all night to further discuss the merits of the evening's mesmerising events, both Graham and Stephanie agreed the opportunity was too good to pass over. As a man and wife so deserving of the gift of a new life, they contacted Helena the next day, agreeing to her proposal should the offer stand.

From there on, the taboo was broken, and the barriers came crashing down. Helena turned out to be the perfect subject to provide a surrogate pregnancy. Throughout the endless medicals and counselling sessions, not one of the many experts they engaged had indicated there would be any physical complications. They were all consenting adults – the last thing to cross any of their minds was the propensity for any strand of emotional fallout.

It had all seemed so perfect. Up to now all Graham had been concerned about were the explanations the child would eventually demand in later years as well as the functional preparation every new parent endures. Yet nothing had really prepared him for this.

As his best friend in the whole world pleaded to, 'Let me hold my baby,' Graham could not wrench himself from the heartbreaking sight of Stephanie, slumped in her chair at the far corner of the room, shattered and broken, sobbing uncontrollably.

Finally giving in to Helena's angst ridden begging, Graham placed the contented child into the arms of his biological mother. Horrified, Stephanie could only mouth words as her throat closed over, making breathing difficult. Deep down, he could not shake himself away from one nightmare question now burdening his soul.

Had Helena deceived him, betraying a lifelong friendship, way beyond forgiveness, in order to legitimately bring this child into the world?

Examining the repercussions of their actions would have to follow later. For now, all Graham concerned himself with was his wife.

Taking her by the hand, he silently led Stephanie from the delivery room, ready to contemplate and discuss what they had done. Both their minds were in need of repair, requiring space to start with a mental clearing. The grounds had never seemed so inviting; logic would easily come to the surface of their conversations. The environment was perfect.

It was time to go for a walk.

# *Flipped*

He checked his pockets – his wallet was missing, and in it, that most vital of clues.

Stumbling in a panicked stupor through a familiar street he had never walked through alone before, Geoff desperately racked his mind, grasping for memories of yesterday evening's sequence of events. Both sides of the road were bordered by row upon row of shops, all firmly closed and secured behind an impenetrable cloak of steel shutters. Without exception, all were adorned with vulgar levels of graffiti. To the casual eye, they resembled a jumbled mess of thoughtless acts of hooliganism; Geoff knew what they really meant though – these were territorial or "turf" markings.

It was Sunday morning, 6.00 am; his local knowledge knew this part of town was still dangerous at such an early hour. Even more acute was his self-awareness of the danger he would be in should he be recognised by a knowing local resident. His situation was exacerbated simply by the fact he was still wearing the same suit he had worn for the whole of the previous night, so, overall, his unshaven unkempt appearance was only likely ever to heap more attention upon himself. Without a doubt, just by being here right now was a high risk. For sure, they would be after him already anyway.

Pausing outside a newsagent proprietor opening the shutters to his premises, he checked his crumpled jacket once again, inside and out, disbelieving that such a schoolboy error of his own making could jeopardise everything. It wasn't about the little money in the wallet, or the harmless stash of receipts that bothered him right now. It was something far more alarming. Once again, he reprimanded himself for his carelessness and stupidity, grateful for the small mercy there were no family photos kept in it all the same.

Groaning aloud as he caught his reflection in the newly exposed panelled glass of the shop front, he knew it was all over. He did not recognise the tatty, scruffy, unfortunate soul whose reflection stared back at him. Obviously, they had already started playing games with his mind.

With a nervous glance, the newsagent asked if everything was OK – the last thing he wanted so early into the day was trouble.

‘What day is it?’ Geoff mumbled, tearing his gaze from the glass.

When confirming it was indeed Sunday, a small crack opened in Geoff’s memory, replaying in blurred slow motion flashbacks from last night’s fateful encounter. Cursing himself once again, his anger and self-loathing mounted as his mistake dawned on him ever clearer.

He had been working on his current assignment for six months, mainly isolated and alone, but with the full knowledge and support of his colleagues and superiors. Specially chosen for the job, due to his impeccable track record in a servitude spanning eighteen years, it was to be the catalyst for promised bigger and better things. Having been a career man all his life, ambition still burned brightly for him, and, upon successful completion of this relatively straightforward assignment, the sky would be the limit. The big time really was about to beckon.

Shuffling on a few metres further in despair, senses still numbed, each step brought a further horrific realization of his current situation. As the amnesia dissolved, the memories started attacking him, remorselessly, wave upon wave. Unable to walk further as the weight of the memories visibly caused his shoulders to sag, Geoff simply stopped and stood, allowing the reality engulf him.

In his line of business, he was referred to as "Stranger". A codename devised to protect his true identity, yet highly appropriate for the complexity of what was required from Geoff to succeed, always running parallel with the knowledge of the very real danger he was immersing himself in upon accepting the contract.

It had all come back to him now. Turning 360 degrees taking in every nuance of his surroundings, Geoff sunk to his knees in despair, a feeling of utter hopelessness enveloping him like a fog. It was all over. His family, his career, and, quite possibly his life, all snuffed out in a few hours of madness.

His downfall began in the nightclub. He could barely bring himself to replay it all, yet there was no alternative. If he was ever going to get out of this self-inflicted mess, then every detail needed to be reviewed, despite his perilous state of mind.

The evening began normally enough, staking out the local watering hole of his target. Geoff was to gather intelligence only on the suspect at this stage, reporting back every week at the designated safe house contact point fifty miles away in a neighbouring city on the county borders.

His target, Karl, was due to link up with him in a pre-arranged meeting. This had been brokered through an extensive network of covert contacts on both sides. Their "friendship" had been fostered and cultured through intense exercises in developing trust and a mutual business benefit, all of which Geoff was highly trained in as a recognized specialist in criminal gang psychology.

Every inch of the operation had to be taken meticulously, as Karl was the most wanted, highly dangerous underground "numbers" operator in the city, and had been for several years. Unlicensed fighting, intimidation, protection and extortion were his particular gifts to society, and right now, his business empire was thriving.

A dangerous individual, who had been brought up and exclusively educated in the ways of violence, Karl had spent half of his adult life in and out of prison for various violent crimes, and his barbarity in order to make a profit knew no limits.

Geoff was tasked with infiltration. He was to collate sufficient evidence in the biggest "sting" operation in the history of the force. For a man of his unquestionable skill and experience, the operation should have been straightforward.

All had been going well until last night, when Karl turned up at the agreed location to their meticulously planned meeting with Angie. Unfortunately, she was something that none of the geniuses in tactical had prepared for. In a split second, Geoff was abandoning his carefully rehearsed scripts, finding himself "flying without a net".

After an hour spent breaking the ice, Karl requested of Geoff that he "look after" her for the rest of the evening, whilst he attended to other business. Feeling he had no alternative, yet sensing a major breakthrough in trust, Geoff agreed immediately. As Karl rose from his seat and made his way to the exit, Geoff mentally noted a further eight heavily built (likely heavily armed also he mused) men gravitate to the same door from various parts of the upmarket wine bar.

Upon Karl's departure, the two newly thrown together companions proceeded to enjoy a full night out on the town, taking in several visits to several further wine bars, a restaurant, and finally, a nightclub, owned by

Karl. During the course of the evening, Geoff had failed to identify what relationship Angie was to Karl. As he warmed to this previously unknown, attractive companion, he allowed his guard to slip momentarily, allowing Angie to purchase his drinks for him.

As a consummate professional, Geoff never lost sight of the fact he was working, and, despite the advent of this unplanned encounter, normal rules of engagement applied. However, he found Angie to be such an enchanting individual, and, for some reason despite his extensive knowledge, experience and training, he failed to make the distinction of appraising her as a cohort.

In allowing his basic instincts to disappear, his request for soft drinks was ignored, and once the alcohol spiked beverages had dimmed his usual mental sharpness, his defences fell, allowing his fate to be sealed. Little did he know, but he had been set up all along. As the night continued, so did the advances of his female companion. Very soon, the rigours of his day job were forgotten.

Still on his knees, head in hands, he could not bear to recall the last of his encounter with Angie, but his memory forced it upon him. Whilst his last ounce of rationale complained there was no way out, he needed to close the episode in his mind before retribution arrived.

Now, his mind filled with crystal clear images of leaving the dance floor in the nightclub, being led through a black door, guarded by three massive associates of Karl's, letting them pass without challenge, back to the rear of the building. He remembered prickles of fresh air on his face as they both climbed a fire escape stairwell leading to yet another, similarly heavily guarded door, and beyond into an enclosed office.

Elaborate as it seemed, Geoff recalled being led by the hand through the dark yet immaculate office, beyond the large thick oak desk, to yet another adjoining door. He remembered Angie deftly flicking her wrist as she entered a four digit code on the electronic lock, and, in a split second, they were inside a large, tastefully decorated private flat.

Remembering that the trappings of organized crime were significant if you could morally live with yourself benefiting from the proceeds of blood money, Geoff was led into a lavishly appointed bedroom; complete with a king size four poster bed as its centrepiece. It was to be his home for the evening, and he would not be spending the evening alone.

So many people were now at risk because of his actions, yet he had no way of warning them. For the first time ever, he regretted bitterly his ignorant insistence that he always work alone without backup.

As he finally gave up hope, Geoff lay down on the cool soothing concrete of the pavement, allowing the early morning sunrise to caress his face. It did not matter one iota that he would bring unwanted, unwelcome attention to himself. It would speed up the overall outcome.

Burnt forever onto his psyche for the remainder of time, what little there may be of it, the city's finest undercover policeman, DCI Geoff Wilkins, screamed aloud at the memory of spending the night with this stranger, who was now in possession of the one thing most sacred to him of all, his police ID badge.

Now it was only a matter of time ...

## *The Weight of the Wind*

It came out of the shadows, riding upon the freezing wind of an angry sea, shambling towards her. In the gloom, it looked like something that had resurrected itself from beyond this earthly world – a grey face under the moonlight, black eyes like eternal holes in deepest space, head tipped sideways, feet shuffling, ragged clothes flapping in the breeze.

Melissa halted, alone and, for the first time, uncertain. Those so-called friends who had brought her here were long gone, dispersing across the desolate beach, rendering her unto the clear night sky many minutes ago. Folding her arms protectively across her chest, she ventured forwards, beneath the carnivorous canopy of the pier end, inching ever closer to the churning, thrashing mass of water connecting with dry land.

Being grateful for having the common sense to plan for the unseasonably cold weather before starting her holiday, she had dressed appropriately for the occasion. Yet despite her thick jumper, jeans and waterproofs, she felt her skin crawling, as if coming alive, shrinking away from the vision before her. She stopped dead in her tracks, feeling the hair standing upright on the nape of her neck, creeping up her forearms.

It shuffled closer.

'It's only a man,' she whispered to herself. Not a ghost or a zombie. Melissa knew. Ghosts aren't real. Zombies don't exist. Nothing like that can affect you. It's all in the imagination of believers.

'You're a trick of the moon. You aren't anyone or anything,' Melissa spoke audibly and clearly now, needing to hear her voice above the din of crashing waves and tortured night screeches of hovering seagulls.

No, this *vision* heading towards her, hand now outstretched in her direction, was simply a man. One of the many unfortunate down-and-outs who ventured to this part of the beach when dark claimed the night as its own. Melissa felt nothing but pity for these poor people, whose lives had taken such terrible twists of fate, their existence resorting to this.

His features were shadowed by moonlight; the unspeaking man was a few strides from her. A sudden realization that she actually *was* alone forced a rapid rethink to her actions.

She quickly stepped backwards, suddenly suspecting that he might not be alone, that others like *him* may also be watching her, and snapped her head around. She saw or heard no one else. Remaining ill at ease, she knew there must be others watching somewhere.

Beyond her line of sight, high above the lifeless pier, hovering on the strengthening wind currents, the gathering mass of seagulls continued their rising, screeching hysterical cacophony. In the six summers she had spent here, never before had such a noise been generated by these all too familiar residents of the resort. Something was bothering them.

How had she gotten into this in the first place? She cursed her pig-headedness and bold declarations as the man slowly closed the gap again, words forming in his mouth, yet no sound partnering them.

Directly above her, the end of the pier funfair loomed out. Silent, foreboding, empty, now it was abandoned and alone, allowing holidaymakers their nocturnal entertainment. Its silhouette cast a deeper shade of dark across the beach, heightening the sense of isolation.

The evening had started well. As usual, she arranged to meet the others underneath the pier, in the usual place and time. Their activities were always conducted under cover of darkness, as their under age, cider drinking exploits were always risky.

Although their group were aged fifteen and sixteen, Anita, the leader, looked much older, easily able to get served in most places. Cider was the favourite, because it was cheapest, owning that wonderful numbing effect quicker than anything else they tried. Always the bossiest member of the group, Melissa and the rest had met here every summer since they were nine.

As growing pains set in, so did the teenage angst and rebellion, and yet, here they all were, once again, inebriated underneath the pier at 'bored – senseless – by – the – sea.'

Only this year, things had changed. Tony, the oldest and sole local, had let them in on a secret. He had chosen last night's drinking session to share the town's hidden history – namely, the night haunting, right here, at the end of the world famous, yet notorious Grand Pier. Not any old ghost either, but incredible phantoms with the ability to mingle with the living under the cloak of common disguises.

Initially, they all dismissed his story with hysterical laughter and cruel taunts, but, as the effects of cheap cider and Tony's mesmerising recount of ghostly events took hold, the laughter stopped, and serious consideration for debate set in. All, that is, except for one notable abstainer.

'What's wrong you?' Melissa blurted to her holiday friends. 'Why are you wasting time talking about this rubbish?'

Following such dismissive statements, a furious row erupted, and, for the next two hours, the compelling reasoning of Tony's story was fiercely argued.

'Think about all those people that died!' he howled enthusiastically. 'It would all make sense wouldn't it? I mean, the world's most haunted seaside pier on our very own doorstep!' His excitement, coupled with the mini hysteria being created was too much for Melissa.

'There's only one thing for it!' she brayed. 'Tomorrow night, we will return, and wait for these so-called apparitions. When they appear, no matter how late, I will personally prove to you no such things exist!'

The eagerness their faces displayed in accepting her challenge was unsettling, however, as an exceptionally proud individual, if not a little too stubborn for her own good at times, Melissa was committed.

Advancing inch by inch, grains of sand whipping around her bare feet, she could now make out some barely audible words forming on the man's lips. 'Yo ... ot ... reeeellll ... aaaaan ... oooonn!' he groaned through a tattered hole where his mouth should have been.

For as long as her family had been visiting the resort, they were known simply as the trogs. It was a cruel, christening for such an unfortunate group, surely the product of the imagination of a spiteful child. Yet, for many years, way beyond the memories of most, this large group of down-and-outs had intertwined with the fabric of local society, broadly accepted by most as being harmless. No one knew where they came from, but everyone knew the place of their night refuge.

Fear forming steel fingers around her slowly beating heart, Melissa cursed the spineless friends who had left her here alone. They fled as soon as the trog appeared. If it were not for Tony's sensational claims that they were the living dead, she wouldn't have put herself in this position. When the point was proven, she would move on, as she had obviously outgrown them.

Pointing its stony grey finger directly at her, shuffling ever closer, Melissa could hear its laboured breathing, as once again, it mouthed the same words, gaining clarity above the maelstrom of noise around them.

'Yorrrrr ... noooooo ... reeeeeellllll ... Triiiiiii ... moooooooooo ...' it hissed, sinister and malevolent.

Frantically turning, eyes blinking furiously, adjusting to the impenetrable darkness that had fallen upon her so suddenly, Melissa couldn't see her friends. She was hopelessly alone, and, to make matters worse, she sensed movement, lots of it – the now familiar shuffling, directly behind her. Then to her left and right. In seconds, it filled her head as if a swarm of bees had landed in her hair.

Dry, rasping inhuman noises followed, quickly increasing in pitch and volume. Several voices became many. Soon it seemed they filled the whole world. No longer could the shrieks of the seagulls be heard, shattering this blackest of nights. The violence of the sea colliding with the beach was just the merest whisper in the background.

In her newfound panic, caused by the terrifying fusion of the ever-increasing number of unseen trogs, Melissa turned screaming, and tried to run. Her legs would not carry her, paralysis brought on by fear. Her immobility was completed by what she could now clearly hear coming from the mouth of the trog, now only a matter of inches away, reaching out to touch her.

'Yourrreeee ... noootttttt ... foooorrrrrr reeeeeelllllll. Yooooooo rrrrrrr a trrriiiiiicccc oooffff thheee moooooooooonnnnnnn.' It said, in unison with unseen others now surrounding them.

Despite her complete paralysis, Melissa felt everything as the trog reached out, caressing the side of her face. She was unable to scream as black soulless eyes flickered to an angry red as it wrapped its arm around her waist. She felt everything as it walked *into* her, freezing her blood as if ice, occupying her soul, invading her living consciousness.

Blissful relief followed as her conscience was exposed to the true identity and motive of her supernatural occupier. At one with the phantom now sharing her existence, Melissa understood everything.

She saw and felt what it was like to be a woman called Susan one hundred and twenty years ago, living the panic, fear, pain and anguish as a family outing to the seaside went tragically wrong. She felt choppy wind cutting into her face as she walked at the end of the pier with Susan's five year old son, Thomas. Melissa tasted stinging tears rolling down her cheeks as she watched, feeling the now living memory of Susan replay the trauma of seeing and hearing Thomas walk too close to the edge of the pier. Felt the crippling skip of a heartbeat as a freak gust of wind rose up from the murky waters below. Saw the hopelessness of the situation as the small boy was swept away in a split second.

In that briefest of seconds, Melissa felt the full effects of staggering despair, hopelessness and wretchedness at the loss of a loved one. The premature taking of ones whose very existence we take for granted each and every day.

Finally, as the tormented spirit of Susan, the lamenting Victorian mother, left the physical presence of Melissa, she conveyed one final clear, message to her young host.

'Stay away from here. They're no place for the young. Dangers of nature will never subside. We'll be here as a warning to others for eternity. Now, go and tell the world about me.'

As she exited, Susan morphed into her earthly existence once again. Falling to her knees, shaking, inconsolable with grief,

Melissa looked up, and, through tear-stained eyes, saw the familiar sight of the trog shuffle back into the shadows, rags flapping in the breeze, holding the hand of a much smaller form – that of a child, a child like no other to be seen, a child wearing similar tattered rags, shuffling with a similar uncomfortable limp.

In spite of the despair and grief she felt, Melissa took comfort that mother and son were joined together whilst forever still existed.

## *The Breaking Point*

So that morning, I could find nowhere to park. Typical.

Despite my rising levels of agitation, I should not have been surprised. In all my years of travelling into the city, particularly this part of it, experience as well as common sense told me I must always observe the golden rule:

'If you don't get here by seven o clock, don't bother coming at all.'

Twenty minutes after deadline, and the game was up already. Continuing to circle the Volkswagen pitifully around the gridlocked sheet of gravel that was the operator's lame excuse for a car park, I filled the air with enough expletives that would make a dockworker blush.

Outside, the sky was crystal blue, the sun hanging in magnificence, energising and enthusing those on the ground. According to the in-car readout, the temperature was already twenty-five degrees. It *was* a wonderful day, yet inside our vehicular purgatory, things were only *starting* to get heated.

Beside me, Helen, my wife of three years, was desperately trying to project an image of keeping calm, yet I knew better. She was burning up inside, her fuse dwindling ever shorter by the second. Relief would only come in the form of a space between two cars, big enough for me to manoeuvre the estate into.

'Why didn't you park it in the other place earlier?' she hissed through gritted teeth, as calmly as she could.

Being equally cutting, using sarcasm as a weapon of choice, my response was direct, succinct and just a little *too* patronising. 'Because, my *love*, God was not smiling down on us favourably earlier and unwittingly directed us to an "exact change only" car park, which, I may hasten to add …' Stopping for a sharp intake of breath, I finished my sentence before she could retaliate '… only had one fully operational machine, and no one on site to help!'

Without even pausing to let the words sink in, sitting stock still, hands folded neatly on her lap, Helen hit back.

'You mean in this day and age – the *twenty-first century* – car park machines don't take cards or notes!' Her eyes widened in mock horror. 'I simply don't believe it!'

'I'm afraid 'tis true, oh fount of all knowledge,' I muttered under my breath, just loud enough for her to hear me.

'Then why did this one let you in? Why did the barrier not stay down?'

Referring to the ticket despatch machine at the entrance to our current location, to the uninitiated, she had a point.

'This, my *darling* is a "pay on foot" car park. It means that a little computer in those barriers knows how many spaces there are, so counts all the cars coming in and going out. I expect that there is a single solitary space somewhere in here, and that's why we've been able to get in.'

'Great!' she chided. 'So we're looking for a needle in a haystack then.' For the sake of peace and goodwill, I chose to ignore her caustic wit, biting my tongue to prevent a response.

Continuing to crawl aimlessly around the rough, loose gravel terrain in the middle of this sprawling place, Helen suddenly screamed.

'There! THERE!' she pointed wildly to my right, grabbing my left forearm, having spotted the deliciously enticing hint of a space, nuzzling between a large red four wheel drive, and a smart executive car.

'Bingo!' Everything was going to be all right, I thought to myself. Inching the car ever so slowly to our destination, our excitement turned to crestfallen despair instantly.

'No!' Helen cried, utterly at a loss. 'Where did *that* come from?' Helen was referring to the second biggest scourge to blight crowded car park areas up and down the land.

'It hasn't come from anywhere,' my response was firm, measured, and sounded much calmer that the raging anguish I was experiencing inside. 'It's been there all along.'

'I don't understand.' She shifted uncomfortably. I noticed her cheeks had flushed angrily, as the first small beads of sweat were forming at her temples. Worryingly, the heat and the situation were starting to get to her already. Without wishing to provoke further emotion from her, changing the habit of our married life, I tempered my response so that she would not get too riled.

'It's a very small car, parked in between two big ones, giving the illusion that the space is empty until you are literally sitting right on it. I'm afraid it happens all the time.' In my heightened state of awareness, I had failed to notice her breathing had become heavier, a little more laboured.

'Oh. Well ...' she grimaced in discomfort a little, '...could you please find a space that is *not* occupied by a dinky toy, so that we can get on with this for once and for all.'

Back to square one. Helen's obvious physical discomfort was heightening my sense of time eroding by the second. If I could not park this vehicle in the next minute or so, the situation was going to turn critical.

'You OK?' I asked meekly, knowing full well that she was anything but OK.

'Fine.' Her response was curt. 'Just find somewhere to park up,' she spoke, repeatedly scratching the palm of her right hand with her left index finger, oblivious to the pain she must have been inflicting upon herself. I took this as a sure sign her rising temperature was about to blow.

'Stop doing that. You will not help yourself or anyone else adopting such methods of self-mutilation.' My attempt at wit was met with a stony silence. Fearlessly, I pressed the matter home. 'You don't even know you're doing it, do you?'

'Stephen, please don't patronise me, just concentrate on parking the car.'

She called me Stephen. That's how bad things were getting. I cannot even *remember* the last time she called me anything but "Steve" or "Darling".

Several more precious seconds of unproductive gap hunting followed, peppered with lots of huffing, puffing and tut-tutting from both of us. Just as I was about to give up hope, making the craven suggestion I drop her off, and she continue without me whilst I looked elsewhere, Helen burst into life with a second miracle discovery.

'THERE! THERE! QUICK!'

As with all highly qualified back seat drivers, she was waving and flapping her arms, pointing them in several directions at once, somehow believing that my senses could comprehend the aimless pointing and gesticulating. A simple 'over there on the left' never seems to be quite good enough.

'I see it.' My confirmation of visual eased the tension, albeit for only a few seconds. Taking a sharp left at the end of the lane we occupied, I briskly poked the now wheezing Golf towards a clear gap, visible and evident across the rooftops of motoring's equivalent to "sardines in a tin".

Upon arrival, my heart sank, and, judging by her face, Helen's turned to stone.

'How can they get away with that?' she wailed. 'Can't we report him or something?' Looking at me, fire in her eyes, defeat creeping into her voice, her *command* was simple. 'Do something. Anything. Now.'

Helen had come face-to-face with the frustrated car parker's worst nightmare. A navy blue Audi had selfishly double parked a bay, its front and rear offside tyres straddling into a second space. To its right, a white BMW was parked inch perfect within the poorly marked line. Quite simply, the space before us was vacant, but our car was too wide to fit.

'What *can* I do?' Despite my outrage, I was not prepared to do anything which involved breaking the law.

'We have to go *right now* Stephen. Do you understand? I cannot stay in this car a moment longer.' Her breathing was heavy, as she clutched her personal satchel protectively to her stomach.

There was no other alternative. 'Then I will drop you at the front. Go on in, I will park somewhere else, and come find you.' Even as the last word had tumbled from my lips, I knew it was a bad mistake.

Tears of pain, fury and fear tumbled down her cheeks.

'No way!' she sobbed. 'I am not going into that place without you!' Her head shook in denial. 'We agreed to this months ago. You *promised!*'

'I know H, but what am I supposed to ...' As I looked into my rear view mirror for inspiration, it came. Gilt-edged from heaven, an angel in the form of a small portly man, silver swept back hair, dressed in a grey suit. Before my very disbelieving yet grateful eyes, he had shuffled to a yellow Toyota parked directly adjacent. In slow motion, he opened the door, fumbled with his seatbelt and started the engine.

'Stay calm and hold on,' I coolly announced, and ice began to run through my veins.

She looked into my eyes, puzzled. The tears had thankfully stopped. 'Wha ...' I cut off her intended speech with a cutting 'Sshhh!' Helen looked over her shoulder, and, taking in the sight I was now locked on to, did as I asked.

Sitting stock still, allowing the overheating engine to protest a little more, my heart leapt as the white reversing lights accompanied the scrunch of gears, and the Toyota was readied to leave the car park. A quick glance around the vicinity eased my fears. No other cars were revving up, ready to die for the cause of parking here.

'Come on, come on!' My impatience was obvious. I did not want another frustrated driver appearing and stealing what was rightfully mine. Eventually, after what seemed like an eternity (thirty seconds at least), the Toyota was gone, gingerly leaving the crowded parking area, and we were in! No fuss, no fanfares, no angels on harps. But who cared? We had landed!

'Thank God!' Helen spluttered, opening the door, levering herself out of the boiling interior.

'Well wait for me then!' I cried as she bolted towards the main building, leaving me to double lock the car. Running to her side, we made our way to the main entrance doors, relief etched all over her face.

'OK now?' I asked, knowing that her radiance was returning with every step she took.

'Everything is perfect now!' she beamed.

With that, Dr Helen Silverton, head of Gynaecology entered the hospital, on this, her first day of work in her new post, at the brand new building designed and constructed by her husband, yours truly.

Kissing her goodbye, wishing her well, watching her disappear amongst the gathered throng of medical experts and patients, I made my way to the conference room. The final construction meeting for the new parking facility could not have come any sooner.

## *Sacrifice*

She stood at the altar, looking at the man who should be her future husband. It wasn't too late to back out. Everything had been meticulously rehearsed, time and time again. She was word perfect, and her moment was fast approaching.

The July sun bore its way into the packed country church, through the centuries old stained glass windows, its splintered rays fragmenting the congregation with shards of multi-coloured light. Such was the popularity of bride and groom; every inch of additional standing room was occupied.

Voices noisily unified in singing the hymn *All things bright and beautiful*, a personal favourite of the bride. Father Peter Murphy had a wonderful feeling about this one; the happy couple were a perfect union, his instinct reinforced by an overwhelming unity and congruence of spirit not experienced here for many years.

Unfortunately, unseen and undetected by the priest, or anyone else in the gathering, one person had her mind on far less happy deeds.

Hazel and Veronica had been best friends since first meeting at the age of four, their first day of pre-school together, twenty-one years ago. From that moment on, when taken into their new class hand-in-hand to meet their teacher, their lives had been irresistibly interwoven, the threads knit so tight, often being mistaken by unknowing others as sisters.

'You are the twins I never had!' Hazel's mother often joked aloud, with anyone who listened. The "quote count" as they affectionately christened it, stopped at 1,000, just before Veronica's thirteenth birthday, on the grounds of acute embarrassment to them both.

Ensuing years of teenage angst followed. Both families lived the full time roller coaster of being there for the girls as they gained their first experience of life's full spectrum of growing pains: Fashion, Music, Pimples, Bodily Changes, Self-awareness and, most significant of all, Boys. Particularly in the case of Veronica, who was widely acknowledged as a vision of beauty and perfection, having blossomed earlier than most.

Her strict father, only too aware of amorous looks his daughter received from the boys each morning when dropping her off at school, had not taken too kindly to the news, when, one evening, her younger sister Rachel teased her in front of both parents about her first proper "friendship" with a rather handsome fourteen year old named Michael.

'You stay away from them my girl!' he hissed. 'They're nothing but trouble, and only after one thing.'

Despite that early warning, falling in love and broken hearts were a regular trauma for all concerned to live through and share.

Academically, both girls were top tier students throughout their learning careers.

Coming through the other side of university with first class degrees, both of them entered higher education as wide-eyed, academic fresh-faced girls, leaving as highly qualified, worldly wise, sought after professionals.

It was not long before career ladders took precedence and men would have to wait. Never had this been a problem for Hazel, who quite routinely had put up with being referred to as an "ugly duckling" when compared to the one person she was closest to of all.

Yet through all of this, they remained inseparable. Moving to the same city, taking similar highly paid jobs, albeit with competing employers, even buying their first house together was perfectly normal for them, such was the strength of their unique bond.

That changed forever exactly seventeen months, two weeks and three days ago – the day Veronica declared she had fallen in love "for real this time", and brought Gus into their lives. Without the slightest hint of hesitation or warning, "Ronnie" as she was known only to her best friend, returned home early one autumn evening, explained everything about Gus, continually gushing that, 'He's the one Haze! He's the one!'

Despite her reservations, such behaviour from Ronnie was not uncommon. Her constant string of admiring beaux, who regularly ghosted in and out of their lives since teenage awareness, were all "the one" at various points. However, the conversation had left Hazel feeling a pang of uncertainty, as unpleasant memories of her own past briefly stroked her heart with ice-cold fingers.

At the time, Hazel dismissed her uncertain feelings as typical best friend jealousy with a hint of neurotic insecurity. Despite her instantaneous reservations, there had been nothing to suggest of the nightmare scenario about to befall either of them. Over the next six months, Hazel saw less and less of Ronnie whilst the relationship with Gus deepened. It became clear that Ronnie was indeed serious about her future intentions with him. For the first time in their lives, both acknowledged they were looking at separate pathways as their futures started pointing in different directions.

29th May is the date Hazel imprinted on her mind for the rest of her days. It is the date that started the sequence of events that had brought her to this point, right here, in front of those they were closest to, before the eyes of God. A point so precarious, she fully well knew that the very fabric of her existence would be unravelled in the next few seconds.

When first introduced to Gus on that fateful May evening fourteen months ago, announcing his and Ronnie's engagement, Hazel's initial shock was paralysing.

Meeting her former long-term, expertly hidden lover of three years was nullified by the need to remain as normal as she could for the sake of her true friendship. Remaining calm and composed, Hazel died inside that fateful night.

Gus had been the one thing Hazel had kept to herself, concealed from Ronnie and her family.

A student of psychology at the university in the neighbouring city, Gus immediately lodged in her consciousness during their first meeting at a shared faculty seminar. The attraction had been mutual, an instant connection of collective minds, bodies and souls. Very quickly, a deeply intense, passionate relationship followed, one that had been theirs only, governed in the knowledge that they would be together forever, as man and wife once established in the "real world".

Following graduation, Gus had taken off without notice, disappearing without trace. There had been no arguments preceding his vanishing act, no life binding plans that could have scared him away. The sense of bewildering loss was matched only by puzzlement and insecurity. Despite the heartbreak, Hazel put her emotional energies into the special bond with Ronnie, deepening it in readiness for adult life. To this day, there had been no others after Gus had departed.

Conversation had been difficult on May 29th. 'I don't believe in the supernatural, but the ghost in my heart has come back into my life.' Hazel was able to share with him when Ronnie briefly left the room. Frighteningly, throughout that reacquainting of the painful past, Gus had not registered the remotest emotion, his face a soulless sheet of set granite, betraying nothing of his past, or the torment it had caused.

As time marched on, it was clear that, despite the soul absorbing love Ronnie felt for her betrothed, the chemistry between Gus and Hazel still existed. In a short space of time, they re-engaged in conversation, tentative at first, followed by waves and torrents. Any spare second it was safe to do so, they would meet in secret trysts, once again hidden away from the world, like a dirty little secret. As much as neither of them wanted it to happen for the sake of all those they loved the most, their powerful union led to the inevitable rekindling of their love affair.

And so it had been until now. Amazingly, it had taken the sight of Gus actually arriving the church some twenty minutes ago that finally convinced Hazel to go ahead with her plan. Outraged and hurt, yet not understanding why, all she could think was that Gus had intended to be with Ronnie all along, and that in some way, Hazel provided him with a link to a past he wished to cling onto, but only on his terms.

All that was about to change, for the sake of her own sanity, Hazel *had* to do this …

Back in the church, Ronnie's intense heart-melting smile told the world she was savouring every second of this, the happiest day of her life. At the altar, Father Murphy, clearing his throat, addressed the congregation.

'Should any man know why not these two people are joined together in holy matrimony, speak now or forever hold your peace.'

Fighting back the tears, the chief bridesmaid took a deep breath. Standing beside both Ronnie and Gus, the man she always planned to marry, Hazel changed her mind in the final split second. Gus could not even bring himself to look at her. Trembling with the hurt, she remained silent, allowing her soulmate to marry the only true love of her life.

Somehow, she would find the inner strength to move on.

## *Blind Faith*

For the last time, he lay on the ancient mattress within the dimly lit room, squinting at the smoke-stained white ceiling. Time was up. It was all over. Loyalty, respect and trust had cost him everything, yet Ardnan regretted nothing.

His was a tale of personal triumph over anguish, overcoming the odds, earning respect and friendship of those around him in this hostile place.

The words of his father haunted him as he lay numb, exasperated and defeated. Ardnan could not help but raise a wry smile. Old-fashioned values had been driven into him early in life, their purpose enabling him to be guided for the rest of his days. These very values had served him well initially, yet ultimately brought about his dishonour.

In these final moments of solitude, he replayed them through his mind, storing the images, sounds, smells and emotions in his memory banks to be called upon for future reference.

* * * * *

His decision to leave home to come here was decided five years ago, driven by lack of prospects locally, and the fables of untold riches earned by groundbreaking others who had beaten a path before him. Such success was attributed to their work ethics, honesty and unshakeable life values. Employers were crying out for their dedication and commitment to success.

Had he remained with his family, a life of fishing or lathe operation in the local factory beckoned. Ardnan wanted and deserved more. An education, respect and personal pride awaited in the faraway land of promise.

When his journey began upon purchasing his airline ticket, Ardnan had his head in the clouds and his pockets filled with dreams. Two long, hard years of manual labour and scrimping every penny from five jobs had brought him to England's gates of opportunity.

Arriving in the prosperous South East, guided by his cousin Mucktar – who had made the jump six months ago – Ardnan found boarding with a room of his own, a small community of his countrymen to rely on for support, helping him navigate this country's complex immigration laws and social security system.

Within six months, he enrolled at the local English language college, progressing to the point of earning the accolade "model student". He found the language itself somewhat awkward, yet such was his rapier sharp intellect, he soon mastered its uniqueness, developing a far superior command of it than any of his housemates.

With the arrival of his work permit, Ardnan had such a confident command of local dialect; he commenced face-to-face interviews with prospective employers immediately. Having borrowed a small sum of money from Mucktar to purchase a suit, he started the lengthy rounds visiting jobcentres, completing application forms, attending interviews and dealing with rejection.

Initially, he marketed himself to higher brow employers. Despite their obvious enthusiasm for his abilities to learn, develop and work hard, rejection feedback constantly informed him too much of a risk existed without previous work history in the country.

Desperate to remedy this, Ardnan commenced three low paid jobs with various local organisations to build up a healthy stable of work experience. Unlike two of his housemates, he carefully avoided illegal underground offers made available, as his wisdom understood he needed a legitimate work history.

Toiling in a car manufacturing plant by day, a public house in the evening, he inflated his income as an early morning office cleaner. He sent what little money he could afford home every week. The timetable was exhausting, but he was determined. Voluntarily, seven day weeks were the norm, so important to him was it to gain approval from his employers. Further enrolling for additional college courses, he knew staying busy was the best way to uphold his values.

Six months later, just as exhaustion with first pangs of self-doubt started scratching his consciousness, salvation arrived.

Despite his punishing work and study schedule, Ardnan continued putting himself through countless interviews with reputable, blue chip organisations, knowing that one day, his time would come.

During an interview with the manager of a major department store, his efforts were validated, triggering the sequence of events to transform his life.

* * * * *

Rising from the mattress, joints creaking in protest, Ardnan took a final look around his dingy, empty room, walked through the doorway and closed his life on England forever. Descending the hallway stairs towards the thick oak front door, he continued smiling at the thought of Monica, and how blinding loyalty to her had been repaid with disgrace and humiliation.

'I'm pleased to tell you that you've been successful!' Monica, the store manager, beamed. 'When can you start?'

Such was the strength of his interview and personality; he had been given a job on the spot! Breakthrough at last!

After his initial moments of shock passed, he hastily arranged start dates with his new, young and highly energetic employer – her smile – it was infectious!

So began his descent into shame and oblivion.

Gratefully yet graciously submitting notice with his three employers later that day, such was his strong relationship and standing with them, all were happy to provide exemplary references.

From the very start, his relationship with his new employer was extremely close. Monica, or "Miss Monnie" as he fondly referred to her, took him under her wing immediately.

During the next year, she personally took charge of his training and development in the store, no other individual ever being afforded such a privilege. He was exposed to the most inner workings of the organization on a daily basis, such was the position of trust he attained through his capacity to learn.

Several times, he attended development courses, aimed at one day making him a manager, just like Monica. Finally, promotion to Deputy Manager cemented his loyal servitude. The gates to his personal land of opportunity were now wide open.

Electing to remain sharing in the same house, the bulk of his vastly inflated earnings were sent to the family at home. Accompanying the cheques were letters narrating his meteoric success – how proud his parents were!

Throughout his success, Ardnan never forgot he owed everything to one person – Miss Monnie. Without her, life would be incomplete. Such a belief in him could only be repaid in one way – complete and blinding loyalty. Dangerously, the closeness of their bond had by now, made him find it difficult distinguishing his loyalties between professional and personal.

Climbing into the awaiting cab, lost in memories of previous greatness, Ardnan instructed the driver to the airport. With him, he carried nothing but the shoulder bag with which he arrived all those years ago. Sighing deeply now, he recalled the final memories of his association with Monica, not quite ready to let go of them yet.

Only when Monica's disappearances became increasingly regular and frequent that Ardnan began losing much of his personal organization skills.

After eighteen months of working so closely together, Monica lost interest in her job, seemingly following personal pursuits during working time, often not appearing in store at all, knowingly using her protégé to cover her fraudulence.

Initially, he took great pride in knowing he could be left in sole charge – even writing home to inform his family of the fact he was in a position of great trust, responsibility and authority. However, as Monica's absences increased in length and frequency, the workload grew to intolerable levels, absorbing ever increasing amounts of mental and physical energy. What she was doing was wrong, but he owed her everything.

The arrival of the letter from the Home Office in early December started the end. His work permit had expired, and, as he had missed the renewal hearing, he would have to return home to sort the problem from there.

When informing Monica, panic gripped them both, for she had come to rely on him as protection for defrauding her employers, just as he relied on her to remain in this position of elevated standing.

Between them, they knowingly agreed to break the law, providing they 'kept to their story, no one will ever find out.' Ardnan was terminated from Company records as a paper exercise only. He continued working in the store illegally and unpaid, usually hidden away in an off-sales area. Monica continued spending much of her time away from the store.

They both decided to maintain such an agreement whilst Ardnan negotiated with the Home Office for a renewal, with Monica acting as guarantor. Such an agreement was honourable and loyal – Ardnan felt happy to support it – after all, they could sort everything with no one becoming any the wiser.

Neither of them planned on the sudden unannounced visit to the store by their

Regional Manager, acting on information that an employee was working in the store illegally. Ardnan was found hiding in the stockroom, Monica absent without permission.

Within three weeks, both had been suspended pending further investigation. In addition, Ardnan had been reported to the Home Office.

Last week, Monica had been dismissed for gross misconduct, a promising career destroyed by selfishness and exploitation of others.

Sitting in the customs office of Heathrow, deportation papers clenched tightly in his hand, he stared at the floor, questioning the wisdom of the very values he had been brought up with such a long time ago.

No longer was he smiling. Returning to an uncertain future and a family betrayed, Ardnan hoped his father would allow him time to discuss the true meaning of hard work and loyalty.

## *Justifiably So*

This is for the following:

Those that know me best, who have frequently called me (in no particular order, yet with some degree of affection):

Grumpy
Mr Grumpy
Misery Guts
Mr Happy

And those who don't know anything about me yet have still sat in judgement, labelling me with the following monikers to name but a few:

Spiteful
Nasty
Vindictive
Someone best avoided
Vicious
Prejudiced
Discriminating
Opinionated
Pious and Narrow Minded

Let me make one thing clear. What I am about to share is not some sort of explanation or justification passage to redeem me of anyone's preconceived ideas. Quite simply, I feel it appropriate at this stage in my life to outline a few of the concerns that have burdened me over time, in the hope my train of thought may educate, enlighten and inform.

Rewinding to the very start of my existence for the purpose of this exercise would be a busy fool's act of folly. However, it *is* worth highlighting that my natural demeanour of challenging the world around me was formed early.

During my adolescence, I couldn't explain why the inside of my head felt it was being continually clenched and released like some sort of washing up liquid bottle, usually whenever I couldn't sense the logic in the actions of others.

At times, my frustrations manifested as anger, and I'm ashamed to admit that I've said many things to my loved ones in the heat of the moment that I never really meant, never truly understanding where such spite came from within me.

Through early adulthood, my aggravated state progressively worsened, so much so, I finally conceded to the wish of my parents, and sought professional help. As much as it pleased the folks I took the plunge, it did not help me control anything. Instead of managing my disgruntled state of mind, the so-called experts inflamed it further. What I *did* learn over that whole year though, was startling.

The source of why I felt like I frequently did was because of my affliction by a common illness – a Social Phobia – and my variant of it was extreme to say the least. I was diagnosed as chronically grumpy.

Personally, I consider myself the greatest cynic on anything and everything the world has ever produced.

Believe it or not, I was quite proud of myself initially, having been diagnosed with a chronic condition, I was still able to walk the streets freely, independently with my mind body and spirit intact.

As time passes, I understand that chronic grumpiness creates horrendous problems socially, despite my best efforts to deal with them. I have had to accept the fact that I am much happier in my own company rather than be with others. Alternatively, whether I like it or not, I have to accept that others often want me in their company anyway.

To be chronically grumpy, or, so challenging of the world around me, life is all about sacrifice. You need to understand that you actually *are* suffering from illness.

Acceptance is difficult. Most of my life, a debilitating sense of isolation has shrouded me in a dark uncomfortable cloak. At times, my disenchantment with aspects of the world we inhabit is so great, anxiety bores into me like a searchlight. There's no avoiding this. Sweaty hands, pumping heart, churning stomach, dry mouth etc – I've had them all quite frequently – usually for trivial things to everyone else.

For the best part of my existence on this planet, there have been numerous times when I have had to shrink back from life itself, weakening or completely severing the bonds of human connection. For those around me, especially loved ones, the effects can be shattering.

However, I am not after sympathy or understanding. As I have said, I simply want to educate and inform ignorance.

My life is perfect right now. I have a loving wife and three adorable children. I feel blessed. Luckily for me, personal happiness has not dimmed my sense of purpose or ability to challenge and question. In many ways, it has worked in my favour.

Professionally, I enjoy a career highly suited to my unique mental skills. Whilst not being the most popular individual working in my organization, I am proud to command respect from every layer of the business. I am recognized at being the best in my field at what I do. And why is that? Because I am grumpy.

I ask questions. It means I make matter-of-fact statements and observations. With me, you get cut through. Because of this skill, not despite it, I have many enemies in business. My life is not in danger as such, but there is a queue a mile long of colleagues who I bet would be willing to pay for a ringside seat the day I take a spectacular fall.

If any of you are one of those reading this now – sorry – it's never going to happen! Grumpiness breeds confidence! When I am not sure, I always hide behind a devastatingly pointed statement or question – it's called the truth.

To illustrate just how this head of mine works, allow me to share my current three favourite pet hates:

1. Noisy eaters in public places.

Why do it? It's not necessary. Bring some manners with you at least if you're a guilty party. And, while you're at it, if you are going to complain about the quality of the food, or the intergalactic price of a cup of coffee, don't pick on the poor overworked catering assistant working long, unsocial hours earning the minimum wage. Politely ask for the manager and yell at him/her instead – they earn more money and are used to it – they won't take it personally either.

2. Bad tempered queue-ers

If you are going to join an astronomically long queue for a rail ticket or a postage stamp – and let's face it, that's normal in this country – accept your fate. Don't spend the next half hour tut-tutting and moaning, only to scream and shout at the stressed out desk clerk when you get to the front. By the way, if you are one of those fools that rubs salt into the wounds by not having your method of payment ready, and spend the next five minutes rummaging through your wallet/handbag – shame on you – people like you are the reason why the queue is so long in the first place. If you want to avoid the queue – be proactive – get organized! You only have yourself to blame.

3. Claim culture

What is happening to this country? A couple of years ago, if a manager of an office or shop felt that one of his team were dressed inappropriately, they would not think twice about calling that employee into the office, reminding them of the published rules etc. For example, reminding a male employee that wearing black nail varnish at work is not part of the dress code and inappropriate would have simply meant that your employee would not do it again as their job was important to them. These days, that very same manager could find themselves having to face a grievance on the grounds of sexual discrimination for having the very same conversation, and the employee likely to be richer after settling the claim out of court!

If this mad plutocracy continues, I fear anarchy is only but a heartbeat away.

You can now gauge why I naturally provoke reactions or judgements from others within seconds of them meeting me. Perhaps you are sat there, reading this, thinking; 'Why doesn't he worry about something *important*, like world peace, famine, child slavery and stuff like that?'

I agree. This world we live in, on the whole, is in a dreadful mess. Global issues really do bother me, and, like millions of others, I carry a sense of guilt and responsibility every time we see distressing images on our television screens.

The reason why I worry in more detail is simple. My worries and grumbles are just as significant, if not even more important in the long term. Why? I hear you cry, sensing your outrage even as I write this.

Because, put simply, if our social fabric continues to erode at the rate of the last decade or so, it is only a matter of time before *we* become the global issue of concern, simply because we have been too complacent for too long, yet no one has challenged the problems on our own doorstep.

I could go on about other really serious issues that are equally painful to me and many others like me, posing such questions as:

Where are the police when the drunks are fighting outside your house at 2 am in the morning?

Who is in control of the young thugs who show no respect for anything other than themselves when they are abusing and frightening decent folk?

Why are not crimes given priority status? Crime is trauma and indiscriminate.

Why are so many motorists being persecuted with speeding tickets when car thieves are killing people on the roads every day?

But I won't.

You see, beneath the grumpy exterior, I am a simple person looking for a simple existence. My problem is that I care *too much*. Something we are all guilty of – I just show it in a different way.

So, to those of you who quite frequently say; 'I would stay away, he's like a bear with a sore head today ...'

It's because I love you, and it's because I care.